I0648892

George Johnson

An essay on asphyxia apnoea

George Johnson

An essay on asphyxia apnoea

ISBN/EAN: 9783337306397

Printed in Europe, USA, Canada, Australia, Japan

Cover: Foto ©Andreas Hilbeck / pixelio.de

More available books at **www.hansebooks.com**

AN ESSAY

ON

ASPHYXIA

(APNŒA)

BY

GEORGE JOHNSON, M.D.Lond. F.R.C.P. F.R.S.

EMERITUS PROFESSOR OF CLINICAL MEDICINE
CONSULTING PHYSICIAN TO KING'S COLLEGE HOSPITAL
PHYSICIAN EXTRAORDINARY TO HER MAJESTY THE QUEEN

LONDON

J. & A. CHURCHILL

11 NEW BURLINGTON STREET

1889

DEDICATION

TO THE LOVED AND HONOURED MEMORY OF

SIR THOMAS WATSON, BART.

A GREAT PHYSICIAN

AND ONE OF THE WISEST AND BEST OF MEN

PREFACE

THE subject of Asphyxia has had for me an especial interest since the now far-off time when my friend and former teacher Dr. Todd directed my attention to the experiments of Dr. John Reid, whom he highly esteemed as an eminently accurate and trustworthy observer.

I have been surprised to find that some recent text-books on Physiology, in opposition to previous writers of eminence, give what I believe to be an incorrect description of the state of the heart's cavities immediately after death from asphyxia, and with this an erroneous explanation of the manner in which the circulation is finally arrested. The subject is one not only of high scientific interest, but of great practical importance; inasmuch as a true physiological interpretation of the phenomena affords valuable assistance in the solution of some complex pathological problems. Therefore, in the hope of exciting more general interest in the subject, I have been induced to publish the following essay in three sections.

A clear perception of the vital mechanism by which the blood is propelled and its distribution regulated being essential for a true theory of asphyxia, I have, in the first section, briefly set forth the now generally accepted doctrines with regard to the physiology of the circulation.

In the second part I have subjected some conflicting statements and theories respecting asphyxia to a critical examination, and I have given what I believe to be the correct physiological explanation of the facts.

In the concluding section I have instituted a comparison between various pathological conditions and the phenomena of asphyxia.

I have not ventured without much thought and careful consideration to express my dissent from the teaching of some eminent physiologists whom I have quoted; and I have only to add that, my motto being *In lucem aspiro*, I shall be truly thankful to be informed of any error, whether of statement or of inference, if such should be found in the following pages.

CONTENTS

———◆———

SECTION I

THE PHYSIOLOGY OF THE CIRCULATION

SECTION II

THE PHYSIOLOGY OF ASPHYXIA (APNŒA)

a

SECTION III

A COMPARISON OF VARIOUS PATHOLOGICAL PHENOMENA
WITH THOSE OF APNŒA

AN ESSAY

.ON THE

PHYSIOLOGY OF ASPHYXIA (APNŒA)

———◦———

SECTION I

THE PHYSIOLOGY OF THE CIRCULATION

IF this essay should come into the hands of anyone not thoroughly acquainted with the most recent doctrines regarding the forces concerned in carrying on the circulation of the blood, the following brief statement may assist him to understand the arguments for and against certain theories which will presently be discussed.

There is now a very general agreement amongst physiologists with respect to the influence which the heart, the large elastic arteries, and the terminal muscular-walled arterioles respectively exert upon the circulation. *Influence of heart and large arteries* The force which propels the blood through the systemic arteries is derived entirely from the contraction of the muscular walls of the left ventricle of the heart. The elastic walls of the large arteries, distended by the injecting force of the heart, react upon and force the blood onwards during the diastole of the ventricle. This resilient force in the walls of the arteries is as obviously derived from the contraction of the muscular heart as the elastic force in an archer's bow has its

B

source in the contraction of the muscles which bend the bow.

The resiliency of the arterial walls, reacting upon the blood during the diastole of the ventricle, gradually converts the intermitting jet of blood from the heart into a continuous stream in the minute arteries and capillaries.

Action of muscular arterioles The smallest ramifications of the arteries, whose middle coat is entirely muscular, are conveniently designated *muscular arterioles*. These actively contractile arterioles, under the influence of the vasomotor nerves, regulate the blood supply to the various tissues and organs. Their action is analogous to that of stopcocks. By the contraction of their muscular walls their canals are narrowed; the onward blood-stream is in a corresponding degree lessened, and the pressure of blood in the larger arteries behind is increased. 'This contraction may go so far as, in some cases, to reduce the cavity of the vessel almost to nothing, and to render it practically impervious.'[1] On the contrary, relaxation of the walls of the arterioles enlarges their canals, thus permitting a fuller stream of blood to pass onwards into the capillaries, and so lessening the tension and blood pressure in the arterial trunks and larger branches.

The muscular arterioles therefore, through their stopcock action, exert a regulating but not a propulsive influence on the blood current. Professor Huxley says: 'While the small arteries lose the function, which the capillaries possess, of directly irrigating the tissues by transudation, they gain that of regulating the supply of fluid to the irrigators or capillaries themselves.

[1] Huxley's *Elementary Physiology*, 1886, p. 25.

The contraction or dilatation of the arteries which supply a set of capillaries comes to the same result as lowering or raising the sluice gates of a system of irrigation canals.'[1]

The discovery of the structure and the function of the arterioles is the most important addition to our knowledge of the circulation which has been made since the time of Harvey. A clear perception of the means by which the movement of blood through the terminal vessels is regulated, and by which it may be arrested, is essential for a thorough comprehension of the physiology of the circulation and for the right interpretation of many pathological phenomena.

The *capillaries* have no muscular fibre in their walls, and they have therefore no power of active vital contraction. They become distended and dilated when the muscular arterioles are much relaxed, and they return to their original size when the arterioles contract and lessen the blood stream ; but the contraction of the capillaries is apparently the result of simple elastic resiliency after distension and not of an active vital contraction. The capillary obstruction which occurs during the process of inflammation, when the white corpuscles especially adhere to the walls of the vessels, is, of course, entirely different from a normal physiological impediment. Capilla-ries

The propulsive force of the heart is transmitted through the capillaries into the *veins*, and so assists to drive the blood towards the right side of the heart. Veins

The small veins have in their middle coat some circular muscular fibres, the contraction of which tends to propel the blood into the venous trunks. The return

[1] Huxley's *Elementary Physiology*, 1886, p. 25.

of the blood to the heart is aided by the pressure of the actively contracting voluntary muscles (the valves preventing a reflux towards the capillaries), and also by the suction force of the chest during each act of inspiration. The terminations of the venæ cavæ and the pulmonary veins in the right and left auricle respectively are surrounded by muscular fibres continuous with those of the auricles; and these terminal veins may be seen to contract and dilate alternately, so as to drive the blood into the auricles.

Pulmo-
nary cir-
culation

The pulmonary circulation is effected by the same propelling and regulating influences as the systemic; but as less force suffices to send the blood through the lungs than is required to propel it through the entire system, so the walls of the right ventricle are thinner and less powerful than those of the left, and, in the same proportion, the coats of the pulmonary artery are thinner and less powerfully elastic than those of the aorta; the pulmonary arterioles likewise contain in their middle coat less muscular tissue than the systemic. The propelling and the regulating forces are so exactly balanced that in the normal condition they work harmoniously together; but we shall hereafter see that in certain pathological states the pulmonary arterioles contract so powerfully as to entirely arrest the flow of blood through the lungs, the resisting force of all the pulmonary arterioles, when contracting simultaneously, being greater than the propelling power of the right ventricle.

Mechani
cal model

The influence of the heart, the large elastic arteries, and the muscular arterioles respectively may be shown by a very simple piece of mechanism. A pump is made of a hollow indiarubber ball with two orifices, to one of which is attached an indiarubber tube six inches long, and to the other an elastic indiarubber tube about four feet long and having at its distal end a brass stopcock. The central end of each tube is guarded by a bullet valve. The end of the short tube being dipped into a basin of water, while the elastic ball is alternately compressed and relaxed by the hand, the intermitting jet of water from the hollow ball, representing the heart, is converted into a continuous stream by the long tube, thus acting like the large elastic arteries. Placing the finger on the tube near the pump, at each compression of the pump the tube is felt to expand and then to recoil. This distension is the pulse, the result of a wave of alternate expansion and contraction of the tube, projected from the indiarubber heart.

The size of the continuous jet from the metallic orifice is regulated by the more or less open condition of the stopcock, which here imitates the function of the muscular arterioles.[1]

The smaller the orifice of the stopcock the greater is the resistance offered to the escape of the fluid, and the greater the force required to work the pump.

If now we substitute for the elastic tube one with rigid walls, the stream of water from the orifice of the stopcock is no longer continuous, but an intermitting jet; so if the opening in the stopcock be large enough to

Effect of a rigid tube

---

[1] This apparatus is described and figured by Dr. Rutherford in a very interesting lecture on the circulation, in the *Lancet*, Feb. 17, 1872. In that lecture he says he 'caught the idea' of representing the muscular arterioles by a stopcock from my observation of the altered condition of the small arteries in Bright's disease. This condition —namely, hypertrophy of the muscular coat of the arterioles—is a result of what I have ventured to call their *stopcock* action, and it will be referred to hereafter.

allow the water to escape as fast as the pump forces it into the tube the outflow will be interrupted. This wide-open state of the stopcock represents a greatly dilated condition of the arterioles, when the pulse may extend through the capillaries into the veins. For the conversion of the intermitting jet from the pump into a continuous stream from the stopcock, the orifice in the latter must be so small as to allow the fluid to accumulate in and distend the tube, the elasticity of which continues to drive on the fluid while the pump, representing the heart, is dilating to receive a fresh supply.

SECTION II

THE PHYSIOLOGY OF ASPHYXIA (APNŒA)

On a comparison of some physiological text-books which Conflict-
have been published within the last fifteen years with ments
corresponding works of earlier date, it will be found that
the former directly and decidedly contradict the latter
with regard to the relative amount of blood on the two
sides of the heart immediately after death from what
is commonly called asphyxia. The term *apnœa* may,
however, be more appropriately used to designate deprivation of air, and I shall so employ it in this essay.[1]

In the 'Physiological Anatomy and Physiology of Todd and
Man,' published by Todd and Bowman in 1856, the Bowman
phenomena of apnœa—there called asphyxia—are thus
described (p. 375): 'When the access of air to the
lungs is excluded the circulation ceases at the pulmonary
capillaries, and on examination after death *the left
auricle and ventricle are found quite empty, and the right
cavities of the heart gorged with blood.*[2] The repletion
of the latter cavities and the emptying of the former

---

[1] Physiologists apply the term *apnœa* to the temporary suspension of
breathing resulting from artificial hyperoxygenation of the blood. This
may be called ' physiological apnœa,' but pathologists require the term
to designate an impediment to or complete arrest of breathing, while the
term asphyxia (pulselessness) is applied to a partial or complete arrest
of the circulation.

[2] The italics are mine.

indicate the position at which the obstruction to the circulation took place.'

The only part of this brief but clear description which is not in accordance with the results of later research is that which assumes that the blood is arrested in the capillaries. We shall presently see that the blood is arrested by the constriction of the minutest muscular-walled branches of the pulmonary artery.

Dr. Taylor Dr. Taylor, in the first edition of his 'Principles and Practice of Medical Jurisprudence,' published in 1865, says (p. 117) : 'As the circulation of the blood in asphyxia is primarily arrested in the lungs, the pulmonary artery, the right cavities of the heart, and the venæ cavæ are found gorged with blood. The pulmonary veins, the left cavities of the heart, and the aorta are either empty or contain but little blood.' In the second edition of the same work, published in 1873, Dr. Taylor says (vol. ii. p. 13) : ' In asphyxia the right cavities are generally found to contain blood, while the left cavities are either empty or contain much less than the right.' He then quotes some statistics published by Dr. Ogston, who found the right cavities empty twice in fifty-three inspections, while the left cavities were empty in every case.[1]

Drs. Guy and Ferrier Drs. Guy and Ferrier, in their ' Principles of Forensic Medicine,' published in 1875 (p. 261), state that after death from apnœa ' the veins of the heart are distinctly

[1] I shall show hereafter that in the very rare cases in which, after death from an obstructed circulation through the lungs, the right cavities are found to contain little or no blood, this is due to the fact that the blood has escaped from the right side of the heart, in consequence of a large vein having been wounded in opening the chest.

traced on its surface; its right cavities and the large venous trunks are gorged with black, thick, liquid blood, but its left cavities are found nearly or quite empty.'

It will be seen that the authors hitherto quoted describe the relative amount of blood in the right and left cavities of the heart after death from apnœa in almost identical terms. I now proceed to show that later writers contradict the preceding statements as to the comparative emptiness of the left cavities.

In 1875 Drs. Klein, Burdon Sanderson, Michael Foster, and Lauder Brunton published conjointly a 'Handbook for the Physiological Laboratory,' under the editorship of Dr. Sanderson, who is also the author of the chapter on 'Respiration,' from which I am now about to quote.

Dr. Sanderson describes the great enlargement of the heart which occurs during the final struggle in cases of asphyxia, when the great veins are so distended that 'if cut into they spirt like arteries.' He afterwards says (p. 323) : 'If the heart is rapidly exposed immediately after death by asphyxia, and a strong ligature tightened round the roots of the great vessels, the organ may be readily cut out without allowing any blood to escape from its cavities. The quantity of blood contained in the right and left side respectively may be measured by carefully opening the ventricles and allowing their contents to flow into separate measure glasses. It is always found that all the cavities of the heart are filled to distension, the quantities in the right and left cavities respectively usually being to each other in the proportion of about two to three.'

According to Dr. Sanderson, then, so far from the

Dr. Sanderson

left side of the heart being comparatively empty when examined immediately after death from asphyxia (apnœa), as described by the writers before quoted, it contains more blood than the right side. Before I give my reasons for dissenting from Dr. Sanderson's doctrine I proceed to indicate that it has been accepted by subsequent writers on the subject.

Mr. Power   In the ninth edition of Carpenter's 'Physiology,' edited by Mr. Power, the phenomena of apnœa are described for the most part in Dr. Sanderson's words, including the following sentence : 'Its contractions [the heart's] become more and more ineffectual till they finally cease, leaving the arteries empty, the veins distended, and its own cavities relaxed and full of blood' (p. 390).

Dr. Stevenson   The third edition of Dr. Taylor's 'Principles and Practice of Forensic Medicine,' published in 1883, after the author's death, was revised by Dr. Stevenson, who, in direct opposition to the description which I have before quoted from Dr. Taylor's first two editions, states that in animals killed by asphyxia 'the cardiac chambers are all gorged with blood, the left as well as the right' (vol. i. pp. 164–5).

Dr. M. Foster   Dr. Michael Foster, in his 'Text-Book of Physiology' (3rd edit. p. 352), makes the following statement : ' If the chest of an animal be opened under artificial respiration, and asphyxia brought on by cessation of the respiration, it will be seen that the heart during the second and third stages becomes completely gorged with venous blood, all the cavities as well as the large veins being distended to the utmost. If the heart be watched to the close of the events it will be seen that the feebler strokes which come on towards the end of the third stage are quite unable to empty its cavities, and when the last beat has passed away its parts are still choked with blood. The veins spirt out when pricked, and it may frequently be observed that the beats recommence when the over-distension of the heart's cavities is relieved by puncture of the great vessels.'

The preceding description is practically identical with Dr. Sanderson's. Then to explain the fact that in post-mortem examinations the left cavities of the heart are commonly found empty, Dr. Foster says: ' When rigor mortis sets in after death by asphyxia the left side of the heart is more or less emptied of its contents, but not so the right side. Hence in an ordinary post-mortem examination in cases of death by asphyxia, while the left side is found comparatively empty, the right side appears gorged.' *Rigor mortis hypothesis* *Dr. Foster*

Professor Gerald Yeo, in his ' Manual of Physiology,' says, ' Both sides of the heart and the great veins are engorged with blood in the last stage of asphyxia; the cardiac muscle, being exhausted, from want of oxygen, is unable to pump the blood out of the veins or to empty its cavities. Owing to the force of the rigor mortis of the left ventricle, and the greater capacity of the systemic veins, the left side is found comparatively empty some time after death, and at post-mortem examinations the right side alone is found overfilled.' *Professor Gerald Yeo*

Again, in Landois's ' Human Physiology,' translated, with additions, by Dr. Stirling, we find the following statement as to the condition of the heart's cavities after death from asphyxia (2nd edit. p. 284): ' The right side of the heart, the pulmonary artery, the venæ cavæ, and the veins of the neck are engorged with dark venous *Drs. Landois and Stirling* blood. The left side is comparatively empty, because the rigor mortis of the left side of the heart and the elastic recoil of the systemic arteries force the blood towards the systemic veins.'

It will be seen that the three physiologists last quoted with one accord, and in almost identical terms, explain the comparative emptiness of the left cavities by rigor mortis of the ventricle. This hypothesis has been framed to explain the unquestionable fact, which is not even noticed by Dr. Sanderson, that at the post-mortem examination in cases of death from apnœa the left cavities are always found comparatively empty and never distended. I shall have little difficulty in proving that this explanation is inconsistent with well-ascertained facts.

Right heart and veins distended

There is one anatomical fact respecting which all writers on the subject of apnœa are agreed—namely, that the right cavities of the heart and the systemic venous trunks are not only *full* of blood, but they are *distended*. Dr. Sanderson, as we have seen, says the veins 'are so distended that if cut into they spirt like arteries,' and Dr. Foster says 'the veins spirt out when pricked.' The distension of the right cavities of the heart after death from apnœa was first demonstrated two centuries and a half ago by the immortal discoverer of the circulation of the blood.

Harvey on execution by hanging

Harvey says (' Second Disquisition on the Circulation of the Blood,' Sydenham Society's translation, p. 127) : ' I have several times opened the breast and pericardium of a man within two hours after his execution by hanging, and before the colour had totally left the face, and in presence of many witnesses have demonstrated the right auricle and the lungs distended with blood, the auricle in particular being as large as a large man's fist, and so full of blood that it looked as if it would burst. This great distension, however, had disappeared the next day, the body having stiffened and become cold, and the blood having made its way through various channels.'

Harvey here makes no reference to the condition of the left cavities of the heart, but this defect has been supplied by many later observers.

Dr. Massey, of Nottingham, has published the following report of the appearances found in the chest of a man four hours after his execution by hanging ('Lancet,' Nov. 9, 1867) : 'On removing the sternum and cartilages of the ribs, the lungs were not to be seen, but were found to occupy a very small space at the back of the chest, resembling the contents of a fœtal thorax, the pericardial sac alone being seen. The colour of the lungs was of a darker hue than natural, especially at the bases. On cutting out the lungs a quantity of black liquid blood flowed. The structure was natural, but there was loss of crepitancy, and but very little air was contained in them. The right auricle of the heart was gorged to the greatest state of distension with blood, and the inferior cava was in the like condition. On opening the auricle a great quantity of black fluid blood gushed out. The right ventricle also contained a large amount of blood. The left auricle and ventricle were quite empty.'

It is evident from the post-mortem appearances that in this case and in the cases recorded by Harvey, death was the result of the exclusion of air from the lungs. With the modern method of execution by hanging it is customary to allow a drop of about six feet from the

Dr. Massey's case of hanging

platform, the effect of which is usually to cause dis-
location or fracture in the cervical region of the spine,
with instant death from the simultaneous arrest of the
respiration and circulation.   In such cases the appearances after death would of course be quite different.

It may perhaps be objected to the record of Dr.
Massey's case that the left cavities had been emptied by
rigor mortis during the four hours which intervened
between the man's death and the inspection.   This ob-
jection, however, would not be applicable to the results
of the following experiment.

Experi-
ment on
a dog   In October 1867 a dog weighing 19¼ lbs.[1] was
killed in my presence by a ligature on the trachea.
The animal continued to struggle convulsively for
about five minutes.   As soon as these movements
had ceased the chest was opened.   The pericardium
was so filled and stretched by the distended heart
that it was at first supposed that the sac of the
pericardium had been opened, so as to lay bare the
heart.   The right cavities of the heart were full and
tense, the left comparatively empty and flaccid.   In
particular the two auricles presented a marked contrast ;
the right auricle stood out in a globular form and had
a tense and elastic feel like an indiarubber ball distended with air, while the left auricle was flaccid and
had its surface wrinkled.   A ligature having been
placed round the large vessels, the heart was removed
and its cavities opened, when two ounces of blood
gushed out of the distended right cavities, while two
drachms and a half only flowed slowly from the left

[1] In my volume of *Medical Lectures and Essays* the weight of the
dog is erroneously given as 14¼ lbs.

side, the relative proportion being sixteen to two and a half.

After division of the large vessels twelve ounces of blood escaped into the cavity of the chest, chiefly from the venæ cavæ and the pulmonary artery. The lungs, which were pale and anæmic, had collapsed to an extreme degree.

It will be seen that the condition of the heart's cavities and of the lungs was identical with that observed by Dr. Massey in the man who had been executed by hanging. In this experiment there could, at any rate, be no question of the left cavities of the heart having been emptied by rigor mortis.

The recently propounded doctrine that the left cavities are full immediately after death, but are subsequently emptied by the rigor mortis of the ventricle, is inconsistent with the fact that the sooner the chest is opened after death the greater is the distension of the right cavities and the emptiness of the left. When the inspection has been delayed for twenty-four hours or more, not only is it found that the right cavities are much less distended, as was first noted by Harvey, but the vital contraction of the pulmonary arterioles having ceased, some of the blood has been driven onward by the elastic resiliency of the distended pulmonary artery and the right cavities of the heart, so as to engorge the pulmonary capillaries, which immediately after death are always empty; while another portion passes on through the pulmonary veins to the left side of the heart.[1]

Result of delaying inspection

---

[1] It is really surprising that recent writers on asphyxia should, in direct opposition to earlier physiologists of great eminence, assert that

Explanation of right cardiac and venous distension

Now the most important and the most debated question regarding the theory of apnœa is this : What is the explanation of the great distension of the right cavities of the heart and of the systemic venous system ? Two conflicting explanations of the phenomena have been given. First, those physiologists who find that, when the chest is opened soon after death from apnœa, the extreme engorgement of the right cavities is associated with comparative emptiness of the left, maintain that this contrasted condition of the two sides of the heart can be explained only by some impediment to the passage of the blood through the lungs. On the other

Dr. Sanderson's

hand, Dr. Sanderson and those who agree with him in affirming that after death from apnœa 'it is always found that all the cavities of the heart are filled to distension,' entirely ignore the evidence of obstruction in the lungs, and endeavour to explain the phenomena by the theory that the contractile power of the heart's walls is gradually impaired, and ultimately destroyed, by the circulation of venous blood through its tissues. Dr. Sanderson says : 'The heart itself being weakened by defect of oxygen, the organ soon passes into the state of diastolic relaxation, before described. Its contractions become more and more ineffectual until they finally cease, leaving the arteries empty, the veins distended, its own cavities relaxed and full of blood.'

Dr. Foster's

Dr. M. Foster, to the same effect, says : ' The cardiac tissues, which at first probably are stimulated, after a while become exhausted by the action of the venous

the left cavities of the heart are distended immediately after death, when the contrary can be proved in a few minutes by so simple an experiment as that above recorded.

blood, and the strokes of the heart become feebler as well as slower.'

And again Professor Gerald Yeo affirms that 'the cardiac muscle being exhausted for want of oxygen, is unable to pump the blood out of the veins or to empty its own cavities.' Professor Yeo's

This explanation of the cessation of the heart's contraction is the revival of a theory long ago propounded by Bichat, the inadequacy of which to explain some of the well-known phenomena of apnœa will presently be shown. An old theory revived

I propose now to indicate briefly the successive steps by which what I believe to be the true explanation of the distension of the right side of the heart has been arrived at.

One of the most instructive papers on the subject of apnœa was published many years ago by Dr. John Reid,[1] who was the first to discover and publish the fact that there is, for a time, an increase of pressure in the systemic arteries when, in consequence of suspended breathing, venous blood passes into those vessels. He expressed his belief that the subsequent rapid fall of the blood pressure was the result of a diminished flow through the lungs, the impediment—as he supposed—in the pulmonary capillaries being also the cause of the distension of the right side of the heart and venous system. With reference to the hypothesis which as- Dr. Reid's researches

---

[1] See his paper 'On the Order of Succession in which the Vital Actions are arrested in Asphyxia,' which was first published in 1841, and republished in his collected *Physiological, Anatomical, and Pathological Researches*, 1848. In this paper Dr. Reid gives a complete history of the attempts which had been made by previous observers to explain the phenomena of so-called asphyxia.

sumed that the circulation is arrested in the capillaries, it should be borne in mind that Dr. Reid's paper was published long before the function of the arterioles had been discovered by the researches of Bernard, Brown-Séquard, and others.

As his experiments were conducted, the observation of the blood pressure was somewhat interfered with by the sudden variations which resulted from the convulsive strugglings of the suffocated animals.

Mr. Erichsen's experiments Mr. Erichsen[1] subsequently, in an elaborate series of highly instructive experiments, got rid of the disturbing element of muscular contraction by pithing the animals, which were then kept alive for a time by artificial respiration. Mr. Erichsen by this means obtained results which were strictly in accordance with those of Dr. Reid ; the main points being, that with the suspension of the respiration and the consequent passage of black blood into the systemic arteries, there is, for a time, an increased blood pressure in those arteries, the result of some resistance in the terminal vessels ; then after a period of two or three minutes there is a rapid decrease of pressure, in consequence of the impeded and finally arrested circulation through the lungs. He maintained that the existence of obstruction in the lungs is sufficiently proved by 'the tension of the pulmonary artery and the accumulation of blood in the right cavities of the heart, as compared with the state of the pulmonary veins and the left cavities of the heart.'

Why right heart is sometimes empty When, in very rare exceptional cases, the right cavities are found comparatively empty after death, this is with-

[1] *Edinburgh Med. and Surg. Journal*, January 1845.

out doubt a result of one or more large veins having been
wounded in opening the chest.

Dr. Sutton, with reference to the great engorgement
of the right cavities of the heart and the systemic veins
which is usually found after death in the collapse stage
of cholera, says ('London Hospital Reports,' vol. iv.
p. 493) : ' When the large veins of the neck were acciden-
tally wounded as in the act of raising the sternum, the
blood escaped from the veins, and the right ventricle was
emptied in two or three minutes ; ' and he refers to one
case in which this actually occurred from the wounded
jugular veins (p. 448).

In the ' British Medical Journal ' (May 7, 1870)
Mr. Worley has recorded an interesting case of clot in
the pulmonary artery which had caused death after ten
minutes of dyspnœa, screaming and struggling. Although
a clot was found 'completely filling' the pulmonary
artery, *all* the cavities of the heart were quite empty.
As from the mode of death it is quite certain that the
right cavities must have been greatly distended during
the last few minutes of life and at the moment of death,
the only probable explanation of their being found empty,
is that one or more large veins had been wounded in
opening the chest ; and it is obvious that the disgorge-
ment of the cavities would be rapid in proportion to their
previous fullness and the consequent tension of their walls.
The spirting of blood from a wound of an engorged vein
after death from apnœa, mentioned by Drs. Sanderson
and Foster, must soon empty the venous side of the
heart, or at any rate greatly reduce the amount of
blood contained therein. It is a well-known fact that
when the right ventricle is much distended, the blood

regurgitates through the imperfectly closed tricuspid orifice.

Experiments on young puppies

Mr. Erichsen in the course of his elaborate investigation made some interesting observations on those young mammals which have the eyes closed at the time of birth, and in which for some days after birth the foramen ovale and ductus arteriosus remain open. The experiments of Buffon, Legallois, and Edwards showed that these young animals survive the exclusion of air for a much longer period than the same class of animals a few days older, in which the foramen ovale and ductus arteriosus are closed. In the former class it is evident that death would not occur from obstruction of the pulmonary circulation, the two sides of the heart communicating in a more direct way than through the pulmonary vessels. Accordingly, not only do these animals live longer after the exclusion of air, but the amount of black blood on the two sides of the heart is found after death to be nearly equal.

Mr. Erichsen describes the following experiment : ' A puppy four days old was strangled ; struggles ceased in nine minutes. The thorax was then laid open and the heart exposed ; the blood that flowed from the cut mammary and intercostal arteries was perfectly black. At the expiration of an hour and twenty minutes the ventricles had ceased to act; the auricles continued to act for nearly three hours and a half. On examination about two hours after the action of the heart had ceased, it was found that the right cavities and the pulmonary artery were full of black blood, but by no means distended, certainly not so much as in older animals that have been asphyxiated. The left cavities also contained a considerable quantity of black blood, but not quite so much as the right side; there was likewise some blood in the aorta. The ductus arteriosus and foramen ovale were quite pervious.'

'Another puppy of the same age was strangled; the spasmodic movements continued for sixteen minutes; the chest was opened four hours after the trachea had been tied. All movement of the heart had then ceased, and the same appearances, as nearly as possible, were found as in the former case, the difference in the quantity of blood in the two sides of the heart being but small. The same experiment repeated on other puppies of the same age was attended with similar results.'

The unconsciousness and the convulsions are, no doubt, results of the circulation of venous blood through the nervous centres, while the principal cause of the arrest of the circulation in young animals with a patulous foramen ovale and ductus arteriosus appears to be, as Mr. Erichsen says, 'the gradual diminution of the force of the heart's contractions in consequence of the circulation of black blood through its muscular fibre.'

Dr. Reid quotes an interesting experiment made by Dr. David Williams, of Liverpool, who states that, ' When the chest is laid open immediately after the trachea is tied during the acme of inspiration, the pulmonary veins soon become empty, while the pulmonary artery continues full.[1] He concluded that the blood is obstructed in its passage through the lungs, and that the obstruction arises from a deprivation of pure atmospheric air.'

In connection with this observation it is interesting

Dr. David Williams

---

[1] Dr. Williams's paper is entitled 'On the Cause and Effects of an Obstruction of Blood in the Lungs.' *Edin. Med. and Surg. Journal*, xix. 524, 1823.

Effect of readmission of air

to note one result of Dr. Reid's experiments as recorded in the following statement: 'When atmospheric air was allowed to enter the lungs after the mercury had sunk to the lowest level in the instrument' (i.e. the mercurial dynamometer, in a systemic artery), 'no sooner had the air acted upon the blood in the lungs, than the mercury instantly sprang up several inches; and when the blood had become more perfectly arterialised, it again stood lower, and the range was more limited.'

This interesting and instructive observation has often been verified by subsequent experimenters, and, as I shall presently show, it is verified in every case of rapid recovery from anæsthesia by nitrous oxide gas.

Dr. Rutherford's experiments

But the most complete and entirely satisfactory experiments tending to throw light upon the phenomena of apnœa are those which have been performed upon animals under the paralysing influence of curara. I am indebted to my friend and former colleague Dr. Rutherford, now the distinguished Professor of the Institutes of Medicine in the University of Edinburgh, for the opportunity of witnessing some experiments performed in 1873, the results of which I will endeavour as briefly as possible to describe. I may state at once that the results, although in some respects more complete and conclusive than those obtained by Dr. John Reid and Mr. Erichsen, are entirely in accordance with their observations.

Into the trachea of a dog a tube was tied and connected with a bellows for the performance of artificial respiration. The voluntary muscles were then paralysed by the injection of curara, and the animal was kept alive by artificial respiration. The sternum and portions of the ribs were removed and the pericardium was opened, so as to expose the whole of the anterior surface of the heart. One common carotid artery was divided, and a dynamometer-tube connected with a mercurial kymograph was introduced into the proximal end. In making all these preparations, much time and labour and great skill were required. Artificial respiration was now suspended, and immediately the colour of the left auricle changed from crimson to purple, the dark venous blood showing through the thin walls of the auricle, and the kymograph indicated a continuous increase of pressure in the systemic arteries. The variations of arterial pressure were registered by a pen on a revolving cylinder. After the increase of pressure had continued for about a minute, the *left* cavities of the heart became much distended; the auricle, in particular, became expanded into a tense globular ball with a smooth surface (fig. 1, p. 24). In the next period, the pressure in the arteries began to fall, and, about the same time, the right cavities of the heart, which had hitherto remained of the normal size and form, began to expand, while the distension of the left began rapidly to subside. Meanwhile, the right cavities became more and more distended, and now the *right* auricle assumed the appearance of a tense globular ball, while the left auricle had become nearly empty and flaccid. The right ventricle also became so distended that it projected above the level of the left (fig. 2, p. 25).

This was the condition of the heart's cavities when the animal died by the final arrest of the circulation through the lungs; but more than once, when the circulation was nearly at a standstill, artificial respiration

Effect of readmission of air

was resumed, and then all the phenomena rapidly changed. The blood, which had accumulated in the pulmonary artery and the right side of the heart, at once passed freely through the lungs, the distension of the right cavities of the heart subsided, and the systemic arterial pressure became first excessive, while the blood was partly venous, and then normal, when the blood

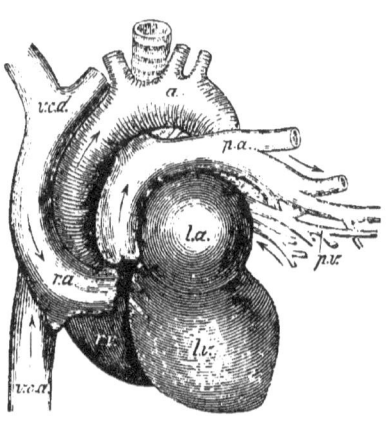

FIG. 1.—Represents the distension of the left cavities of the heart and aorta in the first stage of apnœa (asphyxia). *l.a.* left auricle. *l.v.* left ventricle. Both greatly distended, the former like a smooth indiarubber ball. *a.* aorta distended. *p.a.* pulmonary artery. *p.v.* pulmonary vein. *r.a.* right auricle. *r.v.* right ventricle. *v.c.d.* descending vena cava. *v.c.a.* ascending vena cava. The right cavities of the heart, the pulmonary artery, and the systemic veins are in a state of normal fullness. The right ventricle is partly overlapped by the distended left.

had become thoroughly oxygenised, and its passage through the terminal vessels was no longer resisted.

We have now to consider the minute mechanism of the process by which first the systemic and then the pulmonary circulation is impeded after the respiration is suspended.

Theory of Alison and Reid.   The theory originally propounded by Dr. Alison, and afterwards accepted by Dr. Reid and other physiologists, was that when respiration has been suspended the blood is impeded in its passage through the *capillaries* and finally arrested there.   As regards the lungs, their condition immediately after death from apnœa affords conclusive evidence that the blood has *not* been arrested in the capillaries.   If the blood stagnated in those vessels, capillary engorgement would be a necessary and constant result, whereas, on the contrary, while the trunk and

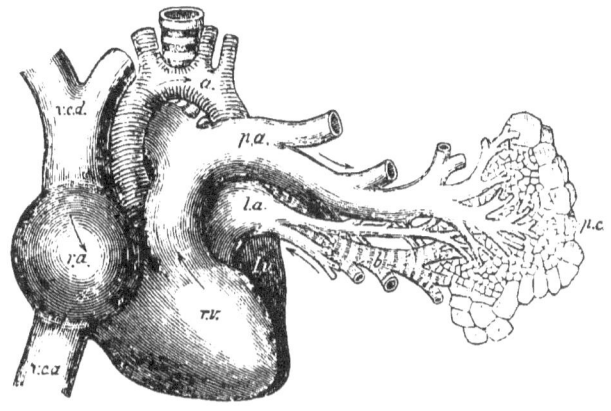

FIG. 2.—Represents the distension of the right cavities of the heart, of the pulmonary artery, and the large systemic veins in the final stage of apnœa (asphyxia). The letters have the same significance as in fig. 1. In addition, *p.c.* indicates the anæmic condition of the pulmonary capillaries. *b.* left bronchus. The right auricle and ventricle and the pulmonary artery are fully distended, the auricle having the form and smoothness of a distended ball, while the left cavities of the heart and the aorta are collapsed and nearly empty.

main ramifications of the pulmonary artery are distended with blood, the capillaries are bloodless, the lungs are usually pale, always light in weight, and in consequence of the anæmia of the capillaries the lungs collapse to an extreme degree when the chest is opened.   The blood has evidently been arrested in the terminal branches of the pulmonary artery, just before it has reached the capillaries.   These terminal branches, we know, are the muscular-walled arterioles, and their contraction affords an adequate explanation of the arrest of the pulmonary circulation.

Engorgement of bronchial veins

Here it may be well to mention that in some cases the mucous membrane of the bronchi and the surface of the lungs are more or less cyanosed. This dark colour is due to a backward engorgement of the *bronchial* veins and capillaries, which share in the congestion of the whole systemic venous system. In some cases the congestion is so great that ecchymoses appear beneath the pleura.

It will be seen from the results of this experiment that the two sides of the heart during the process of apnœa are not fully distended at the same time. On the contrary, as soon as the distension of the right cavities commences, that of the left begins to subside; and by the time that the distension of the right side is complete, that of the left has entirely passed away.

The true theory

We are now in a position to give a rational physiological explanation of the facts revealed by Dr. Rutherford's most instructive experiment. Artificial respiration being suspended, unoxygenised black blood at first passes freely to the left side of the heart and the systemic arteries and capillaries. Arrived there, either by its direct stimulation of the muscular arterioles or, more probably, by a reflex influence through the vaso-motor nerves and centre, the arterioles are excited to contract, and by this action of the arterial stopcocks the blood pressure in the arterial trunks is increased and the left cavities of the heart become distended and dilated, as seen in the exposed heart of the living dog (fig. 1, p. 24).[1] The force which

---

[1] If respiration is suspended when the lungs are collapsed and airless, the pressure in the systemic arteries begins to rise immediately;

distends the left cavities in the first stage of apnœa is derived from the contraction of the right ventricle, and is thence transmitted through the pulmonary vessels. The circulation through the systemic arterioles is impeded, but not arrested ; some black blood passes through the capillaries, and this black blood becoming more and more entirely deoxygenised, arrives through the veins at the right side of the heart and the pulmonary vessels. Reaching the pulmonary arterioles and capillaries, it excites there the same arterial contraction and resistance as had before occurred in the systemic vessels. The resistance offered by the contracting pulmonary arterioles, while on the one hand it tends to empty the left side of the heart and so to lessen the blood pressure in the systemic arteries, on the other it causes that great distension and dilatation of the right cavities, more especially of the auricle, which are invariably found to exist when the chest is opened soon after death from apnœa, and which, in Dr. Rutherford's experiment, was plainly seen to occur during the lifetime of the animal (fig. 2, p. 25). It would appear that, while the systemic arterioles *immediately* resist the passage of imperfectly aërated blood, the resistance offered by the pulmonary arterioles does not commence until the deoxidation of the blood has passed beyond a certain stage, and this resistance, again, is rapidly overcome by the readmission of atmospheric air to the lungs.

If the pulmonary arterioles began to contract, and so to resist the onward movement of the blood, as early as

but if the lungs are distended with air when respiration ceases, the rise of blood pressure is somewhat delayed in consequence of the presence of some oxygen within the lungs.

do the systemic arterioles, death from suspended respiration and circulation would be much more rapid than it actually is.

Some additional facts which were observed during the progress of this experiment are worthy of remark. It was noted that the increased arterial pressure, which commenced as soon as black blood began to pass into the systemic vessels, had existed for some seconds before the left auricle and ventricle began to dilate, and continued for some time after the dilatation of those cavities had reached its height; then, while the distension of these cavities persisted, the arterial pressure began to fall, and it was just at this time that the right cavities, which had heretofore retained their normal size and form, began to be distended and dilated.

The question arises, What was the immediate cause of the diminished arterial pressure which began while the left cavities were still distended ? It might possibly be due to diminished contraction of the terminal arterioles, but this is not a probable explanation. It may be a result partly of over-distension of the left cavities of the heart lessening their contractile power. It is not unlikely too that the heart's contraction may be in some degree enfeebled by the circulation of black blood through its nutrient vessels, but this obviously does not explain the dilatation first of the left cavities and subsequently of the right : a phenomenon which can be accounted for only by excessive contraction, first of the systemic and then of the pulmonary arterioles.

Another probable concurring cause of the lessened pressure in the arteries at this period is, that the contraction of the pulmonary arterioles lessens the blood supply to the left side of the heart before the right cavities begin to dilate, as we have seen that, in the earlier stage, the systemic arterioles contract and cause increased arterial tension before the left cavities become distended and dilated.

The subsequent rapid fall of pressure in the systemic arteries, and the comparative emptiness of the left side of the heart, are fully explained by the increasing impediment to the pulmonary circulation and the consequent scanty blood supply to the left heart and the arteries.

Some physiologists have suggested that the suspension of the respiratory movements might have much influence in impeding the pulmonary circulation ; but Drs. Alison and John Reid proved that when an animal is made to breathe pure nitrogen gas, although the respiratory movements continue, the flow of blood through the lungs is arrested as speedily as when the chest is motionless. Dr. Reid [1] fixed a tube with a stopcock into the trachea of an animal. When the stopcock had been closed sufficiently long to cause a decided failure of the circulation, a large bladder provided with a stopcock and full of pure nitrogen was fixed in the tube in the trachea, when both stopcocks being opened, the failure of the circulation continued to increase. Then a bladder of the same size filled with atmospheric air was substituted for that containing nitrogen, when the circulation was rapidly renewed. Dr. Reid says : ' In this experiment the same mechanical movements of the chest which failed to renew the circulation of the blood through the lungs when nitrogen gas was inspired, rapidly effected that object when atmospheric air was

Inhalation of nitrogen

[1] *Physiological, Anatomical, and Pathological Researches*, p. 24.

permitted to enter the lungs, even when tried on the same animal subsequently to the failure of the nitrogen, and consequently at a more advanced stage of the process of asphyxia. This experiment was repeated several times, and, when the requisite care was taken to procure and employ pure nitrogen, invariably with the same result.'

A similar experiment is now daily performed upon hundreds of human beings who inhale nitrous oxide gas, which rapidly produces anæsthesia with a more or less complete arrest of the pulmonary circulation, while the respiratory movements continue. We will now set forth some particulars of this nitrous oxide experiment.

Nitrous oxide an-æsthesia

NITROUS OXIDE ANÆSTHESIA.—In the phenomena of apnœa with the resulting rapid arrest of the circulation which occurs when nitrous oxide gas is inhaled as an anæsthetic, we have a very interesting confirmation of the results obtained by excluding atmospheric air from the lungs of animals; and, on the other hand, physiological experiments, and, above all, Dr. Rutherford's most instructive demonstration, enable us more completely to understand and interpret the facts of nitrous oxide anæsthesia. On several occasions I have availed myself of the opportunity afforded me by the courtesy of the staff of the Dental Hospital in Leicester Square to watch the phenomena which attend the inhalation of the gas, and I will now briefly describe them.

In most cases, during the first few seconds the pulse and the breathing are quickened, as a result probably of emotional excitement. In the next stage, the breathing becomes slow and shallow and the pulse slower, full and firm. Then, after a period which varies in different

cases from forty to eighty or ninety seconds, the pulse
suddenly becomes almost, or even quite, imperceptible,
the features become livid, the pupils are widely dilated,
there is a state of general muscular rigidity; in short,
all the phenomena of the first stage of an epileptic
fit are present. The mouthpiece being removed, the
morbid phenomena quickly pass away, the features
regain their normal colour, the pulse returns, and for a
few seconds has again a full and throbbing character,
but quickly regains its normal condition.

The explanation of the phenomena appears to be
sufficiently obvious. It is admitted on all hands that,
at the temperature of the body, the nitrous oxide gives
up no oxygen to the blood or the tissues. The gas becoming rapidly diffused and replacing the oxygen in the
lungs and in the blood, black unoxygenised blood passes
into the systemic arteries, and excites, through the vasomotor nerves and centre, contraction of the muscular
arterioles. The resistance thus offered to the passage of
unaërated blood through the terminal arteries explains
the temporary fullness and tension of the radial pulse.[1]
The partially unoxygenised blood, passing through the
systemic capillaries, soon becomes so entirely deoxygenised as, when reaching the lungs, to excite contraction
of the pulmonary arterioles. The resistance thus
offered to the passage of blood through the lungs explains, on the one side, the systemic arterial emptiness
with feebleness or even complete disappearance of the

(margin note: Explanation of phenomena)

---

[1] Some writers have asserted that the full pulse during the early
stage of nitrous oxide inhalation is evidence of the direct stimulant
action of the gas upon the heart; but since the exclusion of atmospheric
air has precisely the same effect upon the pulse, that explanation of the
arterial fullness and tension is evidently untenable.

pulse, and, on the other, the systemic venous fullness
with lividity of the skin. The epileptiform condition is
explained by the sudden and extreme diminution of the
blood-supply to the brain, the blood at the same time
being unaërated.

Rabbits
killed
by gas

If the inhalation were continued, death would occur
from the complete arrest of the pulmonary circulation
and consequent over-distension of the right side of the
heart; and this is the mode in which death occurs when
an animal is killed by the continued inhalation of the
gas. In March 1875, my friend and former colleague
Mr. Hamilton Cartwright assisted me to kill two rabbits
with the gas. In both animals convulsions preceded
death; and, the chest being opened immediately after
death, the right cavities of the heart and the systemic
veins were greatly distended with blood, while the left
cavities and the aorta were comparatively empty and
flaccid; the blood on both sides of the heart being
equally black. The lungs were anæmic and collapsed
to an extreme degree.

It will be seen that the phenomena observed during
life and the appearances after death from the inhalation
of the nitrous oxide gas are similar to those which result
from suspension of the respiration in the human being
and in the lower animals. (See fig. 2, p. 25.) The rapid
renewal of the circulation with recovery of consciousness
when atmospheric air is readmitted to the lungs is also
identical with the results of experiments on animals.

Enlightened as we have been by Dr. Rutherford's
demonstration of the condition of the heart's cavities
during the successive stages of apnœa, we may be sure
that if we could look within the pericardium of a

patient who is inhaling nitrous oxide gas we should see that, with the full, tense pulse of the first stage, the *left* cavities of the heart are distended, and that in the later stage of complete anæsthesia, with a vanishing pulse and livid features, the *right* cavities are fully distended, while the left are nearly empty.

It is evident from the many thousands of cases in which the gas has been inhaled without any grave mishap that in the hands of a skilled and careful operator little risk attends the employment of this anæsthetic ;[1] but it is also obvious that to a patient with a feeble, fat heart the distension of the right cavities which accompanies the disappearance of the radial pulse and the general lividity of the features must be attended with some degree of risk, and the danger must be increased when, the muscles of the trunk and limbs being convulsed, the pressure of the contracting muscles upon the veins drives the blood forcibly towards the right cavities of the heart, and so adds to their distension.

I have been told by a gentleman who has had a large experience in the administration of the gas that on one occasion the patient was so violently convulsed that she was thrown from the chair on to the floor. The epileptiform convulsions which result from nitrous oxide must have for their main cause anæmia of the brain, consequent on the sudden and complete arrest of the pulmonary circulation. In these cases there can be no accumulation of carbonic acid in the blood. The convulsions therefore are analogous to those which

Cause of convulsions

---

[1] The late Mr. Clover, in a letter to the *Lancet* (vol. i. 1876), stated that he had put to sleep more than 11,000 persons with the gas, without one fatal result.

Kussmaul and Tenner produced in rabbits by ligaturing the carotids and subclavians. (See the chapter on the Pathology of Epilepsy in my 'Medical Lectures and Essays.')

Theory of cardiac paralysis
Now, having given what I believe to be a true explanation of the phenomena of apnœa, I propose to criticise the theory which assumes that the arrest of the circulation is a result of the muscular tissue of the heart being poisoned and paralysed by the circulation of venous blood, both sides of the heart being, as is affirmed, equally distended after death. This statement as to the condition of the heart's cavities is in direct opposition to the observation of many very competent physiologists and pathologists, from Dr. John Reid onwards.

Distension of right cavities
As I have already stated, the great distension of the pulmonary artery, the right cavities of the heart, and the large systemic veins is a fact generally admitted. The only probable explanation of this great distension is that it is a result of an impeded passage of the blood through the lungs, and such an impediment would seem *à priori* to imply a deficiency of blood in the parts beyond, including the left cavities of the heart.

The lowering of the sluice gates, with which Professor Huxley compares the contraction of the arterioles, does not flood, but empties the irrigation canals beyond, and an enormous accumulation of blood on the venous side of the systemic circulation of necessity involves a corresponding deficiency on the arterial side.

So great is the distension of the right cavities that the blood spirts from a wounded vein as from an artery, and, as Dr. M. Foster says, ' it may frequently be observed that the beats recommence when the over-distension of the heart's cvaities is relieved by puncture of the great

vessels.' [1] This observation applies only to the right side
of the heart, and it is inconsistent with the assumption
that its contractions had ceased because its muscular
tissue was paralysed by venous blood. The visible contractions of the right ventricle cease when its most
vigorous efforts are unable to overcome the obstruction
in front. The puncture of a vein allows the blood to flow
backwards; thus the over-distension is relieved and the
visible beats are resumed.

We have also seen that if in a case of apnœa the air
be readmitted to the lungs soon after the heart has ceased
to beat, the heart's action is quickly restored. Now this
fact is inconsistent with the theory which I am combating.
The theory is an ancient one propounded by Bichat. If
it were a true theory, when once the circulation and the
heart's action had been brought to a stop the arrest
would be permanent and irremediable, and the disappearance of the pulse under the influence of nitrous
oxide inhalation would be a final and a fatal disappearance. For the theory assumes that in order to renew
the heart's beats aërated blood must reach the coronary
vessels, an event which could not be brought about without the previous renewal of the heart's action. We are
often reminded that *post hoc* is not always *propter hoc*,
but no one requires to be told that *post hoc* cannot
possibly be the cause of something which has gone
before. Aërated blood reaches the capillaries of the

Bichat's theory

---

[1] Dr. John Reid has an interesting paper on the *Effects of Venesection
in renewing and increasing the Heart's Action under certain Circum-
stances*. He found by experiments on animals that when the right
cavities of the heart are much distended, as a result of asphyxia or other
causes, opening the jugular vein allows a reflux of blood from the heart,
by which its distension is lessened and its contractions are renewed.

heart *after* its action has been resumed and the circulation restored by the readmission of air to the lungs. The
true interpretation of the phenomena in question appears
to be that the readmission of air to the lungs causes,
through nervous agency, relaxation of the pulmonary
arterioles; the aërated blood then passes on to the left
side of the heart and soon reaches the cardiac capillaries,
but this is a consequence and not the cause of the
renewal of the heart's beat.

Sir Thomas Watson Sir Thomas Watson, commenting on Bichat's theory,
says : ' There are two well-known facts which, on this
theory, would be inexplicable—the comparative emptiness
of the left side of the heart and the restoration of the
suspended functions by the timely performance of artificial
respiration. The air could never reach and revivify or
depurate the venous blood stagnating in the capillaries
of the heart.' [1]

The renewal of the heart's contractions by the readmission of atmospheric air to the lungs, and their
renewal by the puncture of a distended vein, have this in
common, that the beats, having ceased in consequence of
over-distension of the right cavities, are restored by the
relief of that distension ; in the former case by removing
the obstacle in front, and in the latter by permitting a
backward escape of the blood.

Effect of an over-dose of curara Dr. Sanderson gives very few particulars of the
method of observation and experiment which convinced
him that both sides of the heart are equally distended
after death from apnœa. There is one method by which
probably such a result might be brought about. It has
been found that an over-dose of curara paralyses not

[1] *Lectures on the Principles and Practice of Physic,* 5th edit. vol. i. p. 72.

only the voluntary and respiratory muscles, but also the vasomotor nerves.[1] Paralysis of the pulmonary arterioles would deprive them of their power of regulating and arresting the flow of blood through the lungs. After the death of an animal thus poisoned an equal or nearly equal amount of blood might be found on the two sides of the heart ; a result, though brought about in a different way, similar to that which Mr. Erichsen observed when a newly born puppy had been suffocated (ante, p. 20).

One of Dr. Sanderson's statements is not quite consistent with the generally accepted views as to the effect of contraction of the arterioles. He says, with regard to the contraction of the small arteries : ' The immediate consequence of this contraction is to fill the venous system.' But surely the immediate effect of contraction of the small *systemic* arteries is to lessen the onward current of blood into the veins and to cause a backward accumulation in the arterial trunks, with an increase of pressure there. The contraction of the arterioles is equivalent to the arrest or diminution of the running stream by ' lowering the sluice gates ' which regulate the supply to a system of irrigation canals.

Dr. Sanderson's statements reviewed

On the other hand, the immediate result of contraction of the *pulmonary* arterioles is to fill and distend, first the pulmonary artery, then the right side of the heart, and lastly the systemic veins.

With reference to the enlargement of the heart in the last stage of asphyxia, Dr. Sanderson says this is due to

[1] In the lecture before referred to, Dr. Rutherford says : ' The dose of curara should be just sufficient to paralyse the voluntary muscles. If the dose be excessive the vasomotor nerves are also paralysed.' And he indicates the suitable dose for animals of different kinds and sizes (*Lancet*, February 17, 1882, p. 213).

' the lengthening of the diastolic interval and to the quantity of blood contained in the great veins, which, in fact, are so tense that if cut into they spirt like arteries.' It would, I think, be more correct to say that the lengthening of the diastole, the enlargement of the heart, and the tense fullness of the large veins are all results of the obstructed pulmonary circulation. The engorgement takes a retrograde course from the resisting pulmonary arterioles; so that the distension of the heart precedes that of the venous trunks and is not caused by it.

Again, this high tension of the veins, which also exists in the walls of the heart, is not consistent with Dr. Sanderson's statement that ' all the heart's cavities ' (it would be better to say the heart's *walls*) ' are relaxed.' In fact, so tense are the walls of the right heart that the blood is forcibly ejected when they are punctured; and this high tension is an index and a result of the force with which the contraction has continued until the circulation has been finally arrested by the obstruction in the lungs.

Dr. Sanderson says: ' It will be seen that no very obvious change in the heart and great vessels will occur until the last stage (corresponding to what I have called the second stage of asphyxia) is approached.' From this statement it is evident that his experiments have not rendered visible to him the great dilatation of the left cavities, so clearly demonstrated by Dr. Rutherford as occurring during the first stage, concurrently with the high systemic arterial tension, and preceding the final dilatation of the right cavities.

If an over-dose of curara has deprived the systemic

arterioles of their vital contractility there will, of course, be no arterial resistance and no distension or dilatation of the left cavities of the heart during the first stage of apnœa. Dr. Rutherford was careful to avoid this source of error.

I have thus critically examined Dr. Sanderson's theory of asphyxia in order to show that his statements are not so consistent, either with each other or with the generally accepted doctrines of physiology, that we should be called upon to accept without question a doctrine which cannot be reconciled with the careful observation of some of the ablest and most trustworthy men who have investigated the complex phenomena of apnœa.

It is very remarkable that the conclusive evidence of impeded circulation through the lungs in the later stages of apnœa, which the earlier writers on the subject so clearly indicated, should be entirely ignored by those physiologists who believe that the circulation is arrested because the heart is paralysed by venous blood.

Impedi-
ment in
lungs
ignored

SUMMARY OF CONCLUSIONS

The facts and inferences relating to apnœa which appear to be unquestionably established are the following:

When the chest is opened immediately after death the right cavities of the heart are distended with blood, while the left contain comparatively little blood.

Dr. Rutherford's experiments show that, with the increase of blood pressure in the systemic arteries during the first stage of apnœa, the left cavities of the heart are greatly distended, and this distension entirely disappears while the right cavities are becoming overfilled.

The final distension of the right cavities, with comparative emptiness of the left, is the result of an impediment to the passage of blood through the lungs.

The only probable explanation of the obstructed pulmonary circulation is that which attributes it to extreme contraction of the pulmonary arterioles, consequent on complete deoxygenation of the blood.

The phenomena of apnœa are characterised by two well-defined stages. In the first stage there is systemic arterial resistance, with resulting distension of the left side of the heart. In the second stage there is pulmonary arterial resistance, with distension of the right cavities and comparative emptiness of the left.

The statement that both sides of the heart are equally distended immediately after death is incorrect, and the theory of cardiac paralysis, which is based upon that erroneous assumption, cannot be maintained.

The following experiment, performed by a non-professional friend who takes a deep interest in physiology, would, even by itself, suffice to disprove the above statement. A guinea-pig having been chloroformed, the chest was opened while the heart was still beating; when, as a result of the apnœal condition, the right cavities became greatly distended while the left were collapsed and empty. Here, again, rigor mortis had no share in the result.

SECTION III

A COMPARISON OF VARIOUS PATHOLOGICAL PHENOMENA WITH THOSE OF APNŒA

I SHOULD not have deemed it necessary or desirable to discuss at so great length the subject of apnœa but for the fact that a true theory of the phenomena affords great assistance in the solution of some most interesting and important pathological problems.

For instance, fig. 2, p. 25, which represents the Choleraic condition of the heart's cavities in the final stage of collapse apnœa, is also a correct representation of the appearances found after death during the collapse stage of Asiatic cholera.

The distension of the pulmonary artery and the right cavities of the heart, indicative of an impeded circulation through the lungs, during the stage of collapse was first described by Dr. Edmund Parkes, though he failed to explain the phenomena.[1]

If the following extract from Dr. Parkes (on ' Asiatic or Algide Cholera ') were severed from the context it might be supposed to refer to cases of apnœa: ' The right side of the heart and the pulmonary arteries were generally filled, and in some cases distended, with blood ;

[1] See the chapter on ' Epidemic Cholera ' in the author's *Medical Lectures and Essays.*

the left side and the aorta were generally empty or contained only a small quantity of dark blood. The inference which was drawn from the state of the cavities
in the greater number of cases was that the right side
had continued to receive blood till, in some cases, it
became full and even distended, while the left side re-
ceived little or no blood, but had continued to contract,
in some cases even violently, upon the last drop of blood
which had entered it.' Again : ' The conditions of the
heart and lungs seem to point out unequivocally that in
cholera the blood does not pass [freely] through the
lungs.'

Theory
of post-
mortem
distension

It has been suggested that the great distension of
the right side of the heart and the venous system is the
result of a post-mortem movement of the blood, and
this notwithstanding the evidence that such distension
exists during life, and notwithstanding that, as in cases
of apnœa so in cases of choleraic collapse, the sooner
the inspection is made after death the greater is the
distension found to be. This suggestion, for its un-
reasonableness, is about on a par with the theory that
the left ventricle is emptied after death from apnœa by
rigor mortis (see ante, p. 11).

Effect
of vene-
section

The great distension of the right side of the heart
and the systemic venous system during choleraic collapse
is associated with lividity of the lips and skin and with
a sense of oppression and pain in the region of the
heart. In the chapter on Epidemic Cholera (' Medical
Lectures and Essays,' p. 83) I have quoted several cases
in which great and permanent relief from these dis-
tressing symptoms has been afforded by venesection.

We have seen (ante, p. 34) that when in cases of

apnœa the over-distended heart has ceased to contract in
consequence of obstruction in the pulmonary arterioles,
the beats may often be renewed by allowing blood to
escape from a punctured vein. In like manner, without
doubt, the surprising relief which has often been afforded
by venesection during choleraic collapse is explained by
its lessening the engorgement of the right heart and the
veins consequent on the impeded flow of blood through
the lungs.

Many years since I publicly expressed my conviction
that the arrested circulation through the lungs is the
result of contraction of the pulmonary arterioles, excited
by the choleraic virus[1] in the blood. Most of those who
have opposed this theory have done so in ignorance of
the forces which are concerned in maintaining the circulation. They have been unable to appreciate the fact
that the impediment caused by the simultaneous contraction of all the pulmonary arterioles is greater than
the most vigorous contractions of the right ventricle are
able to overcome. If such critics would first make themselves acquainted with the physiology of the circulation,
and then study the phenomena of nitrous oxide anæsthesia, they would learn how speedily the flow of blood
through the lungs may be arrested by the contraction of
the pulmonary arterioles, and they would no longer
attempt to explain the acknowledged impediment to the
pulmonary circulation in choleraic collapse by the untenable hypothesis that the blood is thickened by loss of
water, and is consequently arrested in the *capillaries.*

Theory of
collapse

[1] The contraction of the pulmonary arterioles, excited by the choleraic
poison, is analogous to the spasm of the glottis which results from the
inhalation of irritating gases or vapours.

One fact alone is sufficient to refute this hypothesis—
namely, that the pulmonary capillaries, instead of being
choked by thickened blood, are as bloodless as they are
after death from acute apnœa.[1] Although, in consequence

Retro-
grade
engorge-
ment of
bronchial
vessels

of the anæmic condition of the capillaries, the lungs are
very light in weight and collapse to an extreme degree
when the chest is opened, they often present the same
cyanosed appearance with congestion of the bronchial
mucous membranes and ecchymoses beneath the pleura,
as we have seen to occur after death from apnœa (see
p. 26).   These appearances, as we have before explained,
are the result of retrograde engorgement of the bronchial
veins and capillaries, consequent on the obstruction in
the pulmonary vessels.

Cholera
and asth-
ma com-
pared

It is both interesting and instructive to compare the
symptoms of choleraic collapse with those of spasmodic
asthma.   The general appearance of a patient during a
severe paroxysm of asthma is, in many respects, very
like that of one in the collapse stage of cholera.

Dr. Hyde Salter, in his masterly treatise on asthma,
says :[2] ' If the bronchial spasm is protracted and intense
the heat of the body falls ; the oxygenation of the blood
is so imperfectly performed, from the sparing supply of
air, that it is inadequate to the maintenance of the
normal temperature ; the extremities especially get cold

---

[1] I have elsewhere explained that the blood-thickening during the
collapse stage of cholera is a consequence, and not the cause, of the impeded pulmonary circulation ; and I have also shown that a similar
blood-thickening, from the same cause, occurs in cases of prolonged partial
apnœa (*Medical Lectures and Essays*, pp. 42, 142).   So great is this
tendency to blood-thickening, as a result of blood stasis, that in cases of
prolonged choleraic collapse or prolonged partial apnœa the pulmonary
artery, the right cavities of the heart, and the large veins often become
more or less obstructed by fibrinous coagula.

[2] Page 72. 2nd edit.

and blue and shrunk; I have known the body deathly cold and resist all efforts to warm it for four hours. But while the temperature is thus depressed the perspiration produced by the violent respiratory efforts may be profuse, so that the sufferer is at the same time cold and sweating. It is this union of coldness with sweat, combined with the duskiness and pallor of the skin, that gives to the asthmatic so much the appearance of a dying man. The pulse during severe asthma is always small, and small in proportion to the intensity of the dyspnœa; it is so feeble sometimes that it can hardly be felt.'

The resemblance between some of the most striking symptoms of the asthmatic paroxysm and the collapse of cholera is obvious. What, then, is common to these two forms of collapse?

In both asthma and cholera the flow of blood through the lungs is impeded by the contraction of the pulmonary arterioles, and this is the immediate cause of the collapse in both diseases.[1] In cholera the contraction of the arterioles is excited by the poisoned blood in the vessels; in asthma it is a result of the partial apnœa occasioned by spasm of the bronchi. In cholera there is a primary asphyxia,[2] the result of spasm of the pulmonary arterioles, and a secondary apnœa, consequent on the scanty stream of oxygen-bearing arterial blood that reaches the tissues; in asthma there is a primary apnœa, the result of bronchial spasm, and a secondary asphyxia, consequent on

---

[1] In the chapter on 'Cholera' in *Medical Lectures and Essays* (p. 121) I have quoted several cases in which all the symptoms of choleraic collapse, except the gastro-intestinal discharges, were caused by a fibrinous plug in the pulmonary artery.

[2] For the definition of *asphyxia* and *apnœa*, see p. 7, note 1.

the impeded flow of unaërated blood through the lungs. In both forms of disease the symptoms of collapse may speedily be removed for a time by measures which relax the primary spasm—in asthma by the inhalation of chloroform, which overcomes the bronchial spasm; in cholera by the injection of a hot liquid into the veins,[1] which quickly reaching the lungs, relaxes the arterial spasm.

Hæmoptysis from retrograde engorgement of bronchial vessels

In the apnœa of asthma we have evidence of a retrograde engorgement of the bronchial system of vessels in the occasional occurrence of bronchial hæmoptysis, and in the more constant occurrence of bronchial mucous expectoration, which usually is copious and prolonged in proportion to the intensity and duration of the previous paroxysm.

Dr. Hyde Salter, in the first edition of his book, attributed the hæmoptysis of asthma to rupture of the *pulmonary* capillaries; but in the second edition, with the truth-loving candour of a physiologist and a physician, he adopts the explanation which I had given, and attributes the hæmoptysis to a retrograde engorgement of the *bronchial* veins and capillaries, consequent on the impeded flow of blood through the pulmonary arterioles. After explaining my theory he says (p. 89, note): ' I believe he is perfectly right; I believe he has solved the difficulty, and his solution satisfactorily explains to my mind not only the source of apnœal hæmoptysis, but, what I never could well understand before, the invariable sequence of bronchial mucous exudation upon any form of protracted partial apnœa; for that which would produce bronchial hyperæmia, even though passive, would

[1] See the chapter on 'Epidemic Cholera' in *Medical Lectures and Essays*, p. 88.

necessarily produce an increase of the bronchial secretion.'

Variations of the Pulse.—Without a competent knowledge of the physiology of the circulation it is impossible to interpret correctly many modifications of the pulse. The two physical forces upon which mainly depend the volume and power of the pulse are the contractions of the left ventricle at one extremity and those of the arterioles at the other. But another important factor is the volume of blood in the systemic arteries. For instance, the small and feeble pulse in the collapse stage of cholera, and during a severe paroxysm of spasmodic asthma, is the result of the scanty stream of blood which is transmitted through the lungs to the left side of the heart.

The rapid change in the character of the pulse which occurs during the process of nitrous oxide anæsthesia I have already described and explained (see ante, p. 30).

When, as a result of disease of the respiratory organs, imperfectly aërated blood passes into the systemic arteries the pulse is always modified. *Pulse of apnœa*

Some time since I was attending, with two other practitioners, a case in which a copious effusion into both pleuræ caused great distress of breathing. The pulse, which had been rapid, small, and feeble, was found at our last consultation to be less frequent and with more volume and power. One of my colleagues thought this a favourable change, but I did not; for I noticed that the finger nails and the lips were blue, and I concluded that the fuller and slower pulse was the result of contraction of the systemic arterioles, excited by the circulation of venous blood.   The patient died a few hours after our visit.

_{Acute Bright's disease} Most valuable information may be obtained from an intelligent study of the pulse in the various stages and forms of Bright's disease.   In cases of acute nephritis, with a scanty secretion of urine and consequent uræmia, the pulse is usually full and tense, a result of contraction of the systemic arterioles, excited by the impure blood. The fullness and tension pass away when the excretory function of the kidneys has been restored.

_{Chronic Bright's disease} The long-continued uræmic condition which results from chronic degeneration of the kidneys, and especially from that form of disease which results in the small red granular kidney, is attended with very remarkable changes in the circulatory system.   The radial pulse is very full and tense, the large arteries are thickened and tortuous. There are the physical signs of hypertrophy of the left ventricle of the heart—namely, extended area of cardiac dullness on percussion, the apex below and external to its normal position, a strong heaving impulse, with reduplication of the first sound and accentuation of the second sound over the aorta.   There is evidence, then, of high arterial tension.   Some years since I was led to search _{Hypertrophy of arterioles} for the cause of this condition by the following considerations : Hypertrophy of the left ventricle without disease of the valves or of the large arteries—a fact first made known by Dr. Bright many years ago—is a result, as he suggested, of some impediment 'in the minute subdivisions of the vascular system.'   Reasoning from analogy, I thought it probable that the impediment is caused by the contraction of the arterioles excited by impure blood, and further, that their long-continued over-

action would result in hypertrophy of their muscular coat, corresponding with the cardiac hypertrophy. This led me to search for and to find the hypertrophy which I had anticipated in the arterioles of every tissue that I examined, in the kidneys, intestines, skin, muscles, and pia mater.[1]

The prolonged over-action of the arterioles has registered itself in a conspicuous hypertrophy of their muscular coat. No kymograph could afford a more certain indication of excessive contraction of the arterioles, with resulting high arterial tension.

I have the satisfaction of finding that the existence of this hypertrophy of the muscular coat of the arterioles is now very generally acknowledged, but an unphysiological interpretation of the facts has sometimes been suggested. Some pathologists, ignoring the fact that the contraction of the arterioles tends to impede the flow of blood, assert that they become hypertrophied in their active efforts to aid the heart in propelling the blood through the resisting capillaries. Another suggestion is that there is some unexplained obstruction in the *capillaries*, and that the arterioles become hypertrophied to enable them to bear the strain to which they are subjected between the obstructing capillaries in front and the hypertrophied left ventricle behind. Such theories as these may be left to die a natural death.

Erroneous theories

There is no evidence that the capillaries, unless when plugged by coagula, have any power to impede the onward movement of the blood.

The tortuosity and thickening of the larger arteries in these cases is a result of the excessive strain to which

Large arteries tortuous

---

[1] See *Medical Lectures and Essays*, p. 694.

E

they are subjected between the hypertrophied left ventricle and the resisting arterioles. It is probable, too, that the contact of the impure blood may tend to cause degeneration of the arterial walls, as a result of which they are more liable to be ruptured by the high pressure to which they are subjected.

Cerebral hæmorrhage

One of the most frequent and most disastrous results of the excessive strain upon the arteries in cases of granular kidney is the rupture of a cerebral artery. The powerful left ventricle then forces the blood through the torn vessel into the brain tissue, the result being a rapidly fatal sanguineous apoplexy.

Relation between albuminuria and arterial tension

Attempts are sometimes made to explain cases of albuminuria by increased vascular pressure. It is highly probable that excessive pressure on the Malpighian *capillaries* might cause a transudation of albumen through their walls, but it should be borne in mind that the tension and pressure within the *arteries* is no measure of the pressure within the capillaries in front. The arterial tension is the result of contraction of the arterioles, and this contraction lessens the pressure within the capillaries, so that, other conditions being the same, there should be an inverse relation between arterial tension and intracapillary pressure. The albuminuria which occurs as a temporary condition soon after assuming the erect posture in the morning and before food has been taken is probably due to defective contraction of the renal arterioles, in consequence of which there is increased pressure upon the walls of the Malpighian capillaries, with a resulting transudation of albumen. That high arterial tension is often associated with albuminuria is unquestionable, but it is also indisputable that in the class of cases in which arterial tension is developed in the highest degree—cases of contracted granular kidney—the amount of albumen is, as a rule, very much less than in cases of large white kidney, which, during the greater part of their progress, are unassociated with increased arterial tension.

There is reason to believe that a retrograde venous engorgement, the result of obstructive cardiac or pulmonary disease, may so distend the Malpighian capillaries as to cause albuminuria, a result similar to that obtained by a ligature on the renal vein. *Venous engorgement*

Raynaud's Disease.—A remarkable form of deranged circulation, which was originally described by Dr. Maurice Raynaud, under the name of Local Asphyxia and Symmetrical Gangrene of the Extremities, is, by the general consent of all who have written on the subject, attributed to spasm of the systemic arterioles. Raynaud's original treatise,[1] and his later researches, which were published in the 'Archives Générales de Médecine,' vol. i., 1874, have recently been translated by Dr. Thomas Barlow. This translation, together with a valuable appendix by Dr. Barlow, forms part of a volume of ' Selected Monographs ' which was published last year by the New Sydenham Society. Referring to that volume for the detailed history of this remarkable affection, I propose here to do no more than indicate very briefly its general characters. *Raynaud's Disease*

The essential features of Raynaud's Disease consist in a local arrest of the circulation, with consequent coldness, blueness, and often dry gangrene of extreme parts, such as the fingers, the toes, the tip of the nose, and the *Essential features*

---

[1] *De l'Asphyxie locale et de la Gangrène symétrique des Extrémités.* Paris, 1862.

ears. There is also a remarkable tendency to symmetry in the parts affected; so that the disease usually, though not quite constantly, implicates corresponding parts on the two sides. Thus the upper or lower limbs, or all four together, may be bilaterally affected.

Recurring hæmaturia

In some cases the local gangrene is associated with that form of recurring hæmaturia which has been designated Intermittent Hæmoglobinuria. This feature of Raynaud's Disease has been discussed in much detail by Dr. Dickinson.[1] In most instances of this form of hæmaturia, although all the blood constituents are present in the urine, the corpuscles are usually disintegrated. Professor Murri[2] of Bologna believes that the blood corpuscles are disintegrated in the superficial vessels in which stagnation has occurred, and that arterial spasm is an essential factor in the disease. He holds that the corpuscles are broken up by the combined action of cold and carbonic acid in the stagnating blood; but the whole subject requires, and will repay, a more thorough investigation than it has hitherto been possible for it to receive.

Misuse of some terms

I venture to criticise Dr. Raynaud's use of the terms *local syncope* and *local asphyxia*. The arrested circulation, he says, 'can be compared to nothing better than syncope, in which the action of the heart is momentarily suspended.' But surely to compare the failure of the circulation resulting from suspended heart-action with an arrest which is acknowledged to be caused by arterial contraction is to confound phenomena which are essentially distinct. The proper term by which to designate

---

[1] *Miscellaneous Affections of the Kidneys and Urine.*
[2] *Dell' Emiglobinuria da freddo.* Bologna, 1880.

the arrested circulation in Raynaud's Disease is *local asphyxia*, a result of arterial contraction.

Raynaud, however, referring to the presence of unoxygenated venous blood in the implicated tissues, calls *this* 'local asphyxia.' The correct designation is *local apnœa*.[1]

Raynaud refers to the demonstration of the muscularity and the regulating function of the arterioles as 'one of the most beautiful discoveries of the century;' yet, with a confusing inaccuracy of language, he in several passages speaks of contraction of the *capillaries*, when, from the context, it is evident that he is referring to the arterioles. It is very desirable to avoid such a misapplication of terms as may tend to perpetuate erroneous ideas as to the function of the various parts of the vascular system.

The examples and illustrations which I have given of the derangements of the circulation which are associated with various forms of disease should suffice to show that a knowledge of the physiology of the circulation—a correct appreciation of the force which propels the blood onwards and of the force which impedes its passage and regulates its distribution—is essential for everyone who undertakes either to construct or to criticise a pathological theory.

---

[1] See the definition of the terms *Asphyxia* and *Apnœa* at p. 7, note 1. The function of respiration is not complete unless the blood and the tissues receive their full supply of oxygen. Apnœa, therefore, may result not merely from an interruption of the mechanical act of breathing, but also from any condition which impedes the due oxidation of the blood and the tissues.

PRINTED BY

SPOTTISWOODE AND CO., NEW-STREET SQUARE

LONDON

BY THE SAME AUTHOR.

MEDICAL LECTURES AND ESSAYS.

8vo. pp. 900.   With 46 Illustrations.   Price 25s.

London : J. & A. CHURCHILL, 11 New Burlington Street.

'The volume is a remarkable monument to the industry, the exten-sive experience, and the wide range of reading of its author. If it stood alone it would represent a life's work of which any man might well be proud.'—*British Medical Journal.*

'The solemnity of language, and the air of conviction which pervade the whole chapter upon Cholera, are very impressive, and constantly remind us that the author's position claims for his views respectful consideration. This chapter alone should win for him an honoured place in the history of medicine. . . . Much that he now tells us appears to be so well established that the world has almost forgotten the energy necessary upon his part to enforce his views.'—*Lancet.*

'The topics are of the most varied kind, their presentation direct and simple, the style matter-of-fact, but terse and dignified. The illustrative cases are numerous and valuable. Those whose " past is secure " will read these Essays with interest ; those whose professional life lies before them, with profit ; we who stand midway will find in them both entertainment and instruction.'—*American Journal of Medical Science.*

'Whilst many of Dr. Johnson's contributions to pathology and clinical medicine are now universally accepted as valuable and per-manent additions to science, and are therefore secure from oblivion, there are many reasons why the form in which they were originally presented should not be left to be forgotten in the serial literature of the past. . . . In republishing his Lectures and Essays Dr. Johnson has been careful not to leave them as simple witnesses of the past. He has added sections and chapters which bring the subjects up to the present date and endow them with increased interest and value.'—*The Practitioner.*

'It is not often that a retrospect of a life's work can bring together so valuable and large a mass of available practical instruction.'—*Provincial Medical Journal.*

'We have had much pleasure in a desultory perusal of the volume, and we feel that the profession owes its author many acknowledg-ments for able work done in the past and now collected in a form easily accessible to all.'—*Edinburgh Medical Journal.*

'It will well repay careful perusal, as Dr. Johnson has the power of linking theory to practice, and many useful ideas will be gained, both from the illustrative cases so freely quoted, and from the author's rules for treatment.'—*Medical Press.*

SELECTION

FROM

J. & A. CHURCHILL'S GENERAL CATALOGUE

COMPRISING

ALL RECENT WORKS PUBLISHED BY THEM

ON THE

ART AND SCIENCE OF MEDICINE

N.B.—As far as possible, this List is arranged in the order in which medical study is usually pursued.

J. & A. CHURCHILL publish for the following Institutions and Public Bodies :—

ROYAL COLLEGE OF SURGEONS.
CATALOGUES OF THE MUSEUM.
Twenty-three separate Catalogues (List and Prices can be obtained of J. & A. CHURCHILL).

GUY'S HOSPITAL.
REPORTS BY THE MEDICAL AND SURGICAL STAFF.
Vol. XXIX., Third Series. 7s. 6d.
FORMULÆ USED IN THE HOSPITAL IN ADDITION TO THOSE
IN THE B.P. 1s. 6d.

LONDON HOSPITAL.
PHARMACOPŒIA OF THE HOSPITAL. 3s.

ST. BARTHOLOMEW'S HOSPITAL.
CATALOGUE OF THE ANATOMICAL AND PATHOLOGICAL
MUSEUM. Vol. I.—Pathology. 15s. Vol. II.—Teratology, Anatomy
and Physiology, Botany. 7s. 6d.

ST. GEORGE'S HOSPITAL.
REPORTS BY THE MEDICAL AND SURGICAL STAFF.
The last Volume (X.) was issued in 1880. Price 7s. 6d.
CATALOGUE OF THE PATHOLOGICAL MUSEUM. 15s.
SUPPLEMENTARY CATALOGUE (1882). 5s.

ST. THOMAS'S HOSPITAL.
REPORTS BY THE MEDICAL AND SURGICAL STAFF
Annually. Vol. XVI., New Series. 7s. 6d.

MIDDLESEX HOSPITAL.
CATALOGUE OF THE PATHOLOGICAL MUSEUM. 12s.

WESTMINSTER HOSPITAL.
REPORTS BY THE MEDICAL AND SURGICAL STAFF.
Annually. Vol. III. 6s.

ROYAL LONDON OPHTHALMIC HOSPITAL.
REPORTS BY THE MEDICAL AND SURGICAL STAFF.
Occasionally. Vol. XII., Part I. 5s.

OPHTHALMOLOGICAL SOCIETY OF THE UNITED KINGDOM.
TRANSACTIONS. Vol. VII. 12s. 6d.

MEDICO-PSYCHOLOGICAL ASSOCIATION.
JOURNAL OF MENTAL SCIENCE. Quarterly. 3s. 6d.

PHARMACEUTICAL SOCIETY OF GREAT BRITAIN.
PHARMACEUTICAL JOURNAL AND TRANSACTIONS.
Every Saturday. 4d. each, or 20s. per annum, post free.

BRITISH PHARMACEUTICAL CONFERENCE.
YEAR BOOK OF PHARMACY. 10s.

BRITISH DENTAL ASSOCIATION.
JOURNAL OF THE ASSOCIATION AND MONTHLY REVIEW
OF DENTAL SURGERY.
On the 15th of each Month. 6d. each, or 7s. per annum, post free.

A SELECTION

FROM

J. & A. CHURCHILL'S GENERAL CATALOGUE,

COMPRISING

ALL RECENT WORKS PUBLISHED BY THEM ON THE ART AND SCIENCE OF MEDICINE.

N.B.—J. & A. Churchill's Descriptive List of Works on Chemistry, Materia Medica, Pharmacy, Botany, Photography, Zoology, the Microscope, and other Branches of Science, can be had on application.

Practical Anatomy :
A Manual of Dissections. By CHRISTOPHER HEATH, Surgeon to University College Hospital. Seventh Edition. Revised by RICKMAN J. GODLEE, M.S. Lond., F.R.C.S., Teacher of Operative Surgery, late Demonstrator of Anatomy in University College, and Surgeon to the Hospital. Crown 8vo, with 24 Coloured Plates and 278 Engravings, 15s.

Wilson's Anatomist's Vade-Mecum.
Tenth Edition. By GEORGE BUCHANAN, Professor of Clinical Surgery in the University of Glasgow; and HENRY E. CLARK, M.R.C.S., Lecturer on Anatomy at the Glasgow Royal Infirmary School of Medicine. Crown 8vo, with 450 Engravings (including 26 Coloured Plates), 18s.

Braune's Atlas of Topographical Anatomy,
after Plane Sections of Frozen Bodies. Translated by EDWARD BELLAMY, Surgeon to, and Lecturer on Anatomy, &c., at, Charing Cross Hospital. Large Imp. 8vo, with 34 Photolithographic Plates and 46 Woodcuts, 40s.

An Atlas of Human Anatomy.
By RICKMAN J. GODLEE, M.S., F.R.C.S., Assistant Surgeon and Senior Demonstrator of Anatomy, University College Hospital. With 48 Imp. 4to Plates (112 figures), and a volume of Explanatory Text. 8vo, £4 14s. 6d.

Harvey's (Wm.) Manuscript Lectures.
Prelectiones Anatomiæ Universalis. Edited, with an Autotype reproduction of the Original, by a Committee of the Royal College of Physicians of London. Crown 4to, half bound in Persian, 52s. 6d.

Anatomy of the Joints of Man.
By HENRY MORRIS, Surgeon to, and Lecturer on Anatomy and Practical Surgery at, the Middlesex Hospital. 8vo, with 44 Lithographic Plates (several being coloured) and 13 Wood Engravings, 16s.

Manual of the Dissection of the Human Body.
By LUTHER HOLDEN, Consulting Surgeon to St. Bartholomew's Hospital. Edited by JOHN LANGTON, F.R.C.S., Surgeon to, and Lecturer on Anatomy at, St. Bartholomew's Hospital. Fifth Edition. 8vo, with 208 Engravings. 20s.

By the same Author.

Human Osteology.
Seventh Edition, edited by CHARLES STEWART, Conservator of the Museum R.C.S., and R. W. REID, M.D., F.R.C.S., Lecturer on Anatomy at St. Thomas's Hospital. 8vo, with 59 Lithographic Plates and 75 Engravings. 16s.

Also.

Landmarks, Medical and Surgical.
Fourth Edition. 8vo, 3s. 6d.

The Student's Guide to Surgical Anatomy.
By EDWARD BELLAMY, F.R.C.S. and Member of the Board of Examiners. Third Edition. Fcap. 8vo, with 81 Engravings. 7s. 6d.

Diagrams of the Nerves of the Human Body,
exhibiting their Origin, Divisions, and Connections, with their Distribution to the Various Regions of the Cutaneous Surface, and to all the Muscles. By W. H. FLOWER, C.B., F.R.S., F.R.C.S. Third Edition, with 6 Plates. Royal 4to, 12s.

General Pathology:

An Introduction to. By JOHN BLAND SUTTON, F.R.C.S., Sir E. Wilson Lecturer on Pathology, R.C.S.; Assistant Surgeon to, and Lecturer on Anatomy at, Middlesex Hospital. 8vo, with 149 Engravings, 14s.

Atlas of Pathological Anatomy.

By Dr. LANCEREAUX. Translated by W. S. GREENFIELD, M.D., Professor of Pathology in the University of Edinburgh. Imp. 8vo, with 70 Coloured Plates, £5 5s.

A Manual of Pathological Anatomy.

By C. HANDFIELD JONES, M.B., F.R.S., and E. H. SIEVEKING, M.D., F.R.C.P. Edited by J. F. PAYNE, M.D., F.R.C.P., Lecturer on General Pathology at St. Thomas's Hospital. Second Edition. Crown 8vo, with 195 Engravings, 16s.

Post-mortem Examinations:

A Description and Explanation of the Method of Performing them, with especial reference to Medico-Legal Practice. By Prof. VIRCHOW. Translated by Dr. T. P. SMITH. Second Edition. Fcap. 8vo, with 4 Plates, 3s. 6d.

The Human Brain:

Histological and Coarse Methods of Research. A Manual for Students and Asylum Medical Officers. By W. BEVAN LEWIS, L.R.C.P. Lond., Medical Superintendent, West Riding Lunatic Asylum. 8vo, with Wood Engravings and Photographs, 8s.

Manual of Physiology:

For the use of Junior Students of Medicine. By GERALD F. YEO, M.D., F.R.C.S., Professor of Physiology in King's College, London. Second Edition. Crown 8vo, with 318 Engravings, 14s.

Principles of Human Physiology.

By W. B. CARPENTER, C.B., M.D., F.R.S. Ninth Edition. By HENRY POWER, M.B., F.R.C.S. 8vo, with 3 Steel Plates and 377 Wood Engravings, 31s. 6d.

Elementary Practical Biology:

Vegetable. By THOMAS W. SHORE, M.D., B.Sc. Lond., Lecturer on Comparative Anatomy at St. Bartholomew's Hospital. 8vo, 6s.

A Text-Book of Medical Physics,

for Students and Practitioners. By J. C. DRAPER, M.D., LL.D., Professor of Physics in the University of New York. With 377 Engravings. 8vo, 18s.

Medical Jurisprudence:

Its Principles and Practice. By ALFRED S. TAYLOR, M.D., F.R.C.P., F.R.S. Third Edition, by THOMAS STEVENSON, M.D., F.R.C.P., Lecturer on Medical Jurisprudence at Guy's Hospital. 2 vols. 8vo, with 188 Engravings, 31s. 6d.

By the same Authors.

A Manual of Medical Jurisprudence.

Eleventh Edition. Crown 8vo, with 56 Engravings, 14s.

Also.

Poisons,

In Relation to Medical Jurisprudence and Medicine. Third Edition. Crown 8vo, with 104 Engravings, 16s.

Lectures on Medical Jurisprudence.

By FRANCIS OGSTON, M.D., late Professor in the University of Aberdeen. Edited by FRANCIS OGSTON, Jun., M.D. 8vo, with 12 Copper Plates, 18s.

The Student's Guide to Medical Jurisprudence.

By JOHN ABERCROMBIE, M.D., F.R.C.P., Lecturer on Forensic Medicine to Charing Cross Hospital. Fcap. 8vo, 7s. 6d.

Microscopical Examination of Drinking Water and of Air.

By J. D. MACDONALD, M.D., F.R.S., Ex Professor of Naval Hygiene in the Army Medical School. Second Edition. 8vo, with 25 Plates, 7s. 6d.

Pay Hospitals and Paying Wards throughout the World.

By HENRY C. BURDETT. 8vo, 7s.

By the same Author.

Cottage Hospitals — General, Fever, and Convalescent:

Their Progress, Management, and Work. Second Edition, with many Plans and Illustrations. Crown 8vo, 14s.

Hospitals, Infirmaries, and Dispensaries:

Their Construction, Interior Arrangement, and Management; with Descriptions of existing Institutions, and 74 Illustrations. By F. OPPERT, M.D., M.R.C.P.L. Second Edition. Royal 8vo, 12s.

Hospital Construction and Management.

By F. J. MOUAT, M.D., Local Government Board Inspector, and H. SAXON SNELL, Fell. Roy. Inst. Brit. Architects. In 2 Parts, 4to, 15s. each; or, the whole work bound in half calf, with large Map, 54 Lithographic Plates, and 27 Woodcuts, 35s.

Public Health Reports.

By Sir JOHN SIMON, C.B., F.R.S. Edited by EDWARD SEATON, M.D., F.R.C.P. 2 vols. 8vo, with Portrait, 36s.

A Manual of Practical Hygiene.
By E. A. PARKES, M.D., F.R.S. Seventh Edition, by F. DE CHAUMONT, M.D., F.R.S., Professor of Military Hygiene in the Army Medical School. 8vo, with 9 Plates and 101 Engravings, 18s.

A Handbook of Hygiene and Sanitary Science.
By GEO. WILSON, M.A., M.D., F.R.S.E., Medical Officer of Health for Mid-Warwickshire. Sixth Edition. Crown 8vo, with Engravings. 10s. 6d.

By the same Author.

Healthy Life and Healthy Dwellings:
A Guide to Personal and Domestic Hygiene. Fcap. 8vo, 5s.

Sanitary Examinations
Of Water, Air, and Food. A Vade-Mecum for the Medical Officer of Health. By CORNELIUS B. FOX, M.D., F.R.C.P. Second Edition. Crown 8vo, with 110 Engravings, 12s. 6d.

Epidemic Influences:
Epidemiological Aspects of Yellow Fever and of Cholera. The Milroy Lectures. By ROBERT LAWSON, LL.D., Inspector-General of Hospitals. 8vo, with Maps, Diagrams, &c., 6s.

Detection of Colour-Blindness and Imperfect Eyesight.
By CHARLES ROBERTS, F.R.C.S. Second Edition. 8vo, with a Table of Coloured Wools, and Sheet of Test-types, 5s.

Illustrations of the Influence of the Mind upon the Body in Health and Disease:
Designed to elucidate the Action of the Imagination. By D. H. TUKE, M.D., F.R.C.P., LL.D. Second Edition. 2 vols. crown 8vo, 15s.

By the same Author.

Sleep-Walking and Hypnotism.
8vo, 5s.

A Manual of Psychological Medicine.
With an Appendix of Cases. By JOHN C. BUCKNILL, M.D., F.R.S., and D. HACK TUKE, M.D., F.R.C.P. Fourth Edition. 8vo, with 12 Plates (30 Figures) and Engravings, 25s.

Mental Affections of Childhood and Youth
(Lettsomian Lectures for 1887, &c.). By J. LANGDON DOWN, M.D., F.R.C.P., Senior Physician to the London Hospital. 8vo, 6s.

Mental Diseases:
Clinical Lectures. By T. S. CLOUSTON, M.D., F.R.C.P. Edin., Lecturer on Mental Diseases in the University of Edinburgh. Second Edition. Crown 8vo, with 8 Plates (6 Coloured), 12s. 6d.

Private Treatment of the Insane as Single Patients.
By EDWARD EAST, M.R.C.S., L.S.A. Crown 8vo, 2s. 6d.

Manual of Midwifery.
By ALFRED L. GALABIN, M.A., M.D., F.R.C.P., Obstetric Physician to, and Lecturer on Midwifery, &c. at, Guy's Hospital. Crown 8vo, with 227 Engravings, 15s.

The Student's Guide to the Practice of Midwifery.
By D. LLOYD ROBERTS, M.D., F.R.C.P., Lecturer on Clinical Midwifery and Diseases of Women at the Owens College; Obstetric Physician to the Manchester Royal Infirmary. Third Edition. Fcap. 8vo, with 2 Coloured Plates and 127 Wood Engravings, 7s. 6d.

Lectures on Obstetric Operations:
Including the Treatment of Hæmorrhage, and forming a Guide to the Management of Difficult Labour. By ROBERT BARNES, M.D., F.R.C.P., Consulting Obstetric Physician to St. George's Hospital. Fourth Edition. 8vo, with 121 Engravings, 12s. 6d.

By the same Author.

A Clinical History of Medical and Surgical Diseases of Women.
Second Edition. 8vo, with 181 Engravings, 28s.

Clinical Lectures on Diseases of Women:
Delivered in St. Bartholomew's Hospital, by J. MATTHEWS DUNCAN, M.D., LL.D., F.R.S. Third Edition. 8vo, 16s.

Notes on Diseases of Women:
Specially designed to assist the Student in preparing for Examination. By J. J. REYNOLDS, L.R.C.P., M.R.C.S. Third Edition. Fcap. 8vo, 2s. 6d.

By the same Author.

Notes on Midwifery:
Specially designed for Students preparing for Examination. Second Edition. Fcap. 8vo, with 15 Engravings, 4s.

A Manual of Obstetrics.
By A. F. A. KING, A.M., M.D., Professor of Obstetrics, &c., in the Columbian University, Washington, and the University of Vermont. Third Edition. Crown 8vo, with 102 Engravings, 8s.

Intra-Uterine Death:
(Pathology of). Being the Lumleian Lectures, 1887. By WILLIAM O. PRIESTLEY, M.D., F.R.C.P., LL.D., Consulting Physician to King's College Hospital. 8vo, with 3 Coloured Plates and 17 Engravings, 7s. 6d.

The Student's Guide to the Diseases of Women.

By ALFRED L. GALABIN, M.D., F.R.C.P., Obstetric Physician to Guy's Hospital. Fourth Edition. Fcap. 8vo, with 94 Engravings, 7s. 6d.

West on the Diseases of Women.

Fourth Edition, revised by the Author, with numerous Additions by J. MATTHEWS DUNCAN, M.D., F.R.C.P., F.R.S.E., Obstetric Physician to St. Bartholomew's Hospital. 8vo, 16s.

Obstetric Aphorisms:

For the Use of Students commencing Midwifery Practice. By JOSEPH G. SWAYNE, M.D. Eighth Edition. Fcap. 8vo, with Engravings, 3s. 6d.

Handbook of Midwifery for Midwives:

By J. E. BURTON, L.R.C.P. Lond., Surgeon to the Hospital for Women, Liverpool. Second Edition. With Engravings. Fcap. 8vo, 6s.

A Handbook of Uterine Therapeutics,

and of Diseases of Women. By E. J. TILT, M.D., M.R.C.P. Fourth Edition. Post 8vo, 10s.

By the same Author.

The Change of Life

In Health and Disease: A Clinical Treatise on the Diseases of the Nervous System incidental to Women at the Decline of Life. Fourth Edition. 8vo, 10s. 6d.

Diseases of the Uterus, Ovaries, and Fallopian Tubes:

A Practical Treatise by A. COURTY, Professor of Clinical Surgery, Montpellier. Translated from Third Edition by his Pupil, AGNES McLAREN, M.D., M.K.Q.C.P.I., with Preface by J. MATTHEWS DUNCAN, M.D., F.R.C.P. 8vo, with 424 Engravings, 24s.

Gynæcological Operations:

(Handbook of). By ALBAN H. G. DORAN, F.R.C.S., Surgeon to the Samaritan Hospital. 8vo, with 167 Engravings, 15s.

The Female Pelvic Organs:

Their Surgery, Surgical Pathology, and Surgical Anatomy. In a Series of Coloured Plates taken from Nature; with Commentaries, Notes, and Cases. By HENRY SAVAGE, M.D., F.R.C.S., Consulting Officer of the Samaritan Free Hospital. Fifth Edition. Roy. 4to, with 17 Lithographic Plates (15 coloured) and 52 Woodcuts, £1 15s.

A Practical Treatise on the Diseases of Women.

By T. GAILLARD THOMAS, M.D., Professor of Diseases of Women in the College of Physicians and Surgeons, New York. Fifth Edition. Roy. 8vo, with 266 Engravings, 25s.

Diseases and Accidents

Incident to Women, and the Practice of Medicine and Surgery applied to them. By W. H. BYFORD, A.M., M.D., Professor of Gynæcology in Rush Medical College, and HENRY T. BYFORD, M.D., Surgeon to the Woman's Hospital, Chicago. Fourth Edition. 8vo, with 306 Engravings, 25s.

Abdominal Surgery.

By J. GREIG SMITH, M.A., F.R.S.E., Surgeon to the Bristol Royal Infirmary and Lecturer on Surgery in the Bristol Medical School. Second Edition. 8vo, with 79 Engravings, 21s.

The Student's Guide to Diseases of Children.

By JAS. F. GOODHART, M.D., F.R.C.P., Physician to Guy's Hospital, and to the Evelina Hospital for Sick Children. Third Edition. Fcap. 8vo, 10s. 6d.

Diseases of Children.

For Practitioners and Students. By W. H. DAY, M.D., Physician to the Samaritan Hospital. Second Edition. Crown 8vo, 12s. 6d.

A Practical Treatise on Disease in Children.

By EUSTACE SMITH, M.D., Physician to the King of the Belgians, Physician to the East London Hospital for Children. 8vo, 22s.

By the same Author.

Clinical Studies of Disease in Children.

Second Edition. Post 8vo, 7s. 6d. *Also,*

The Wasting Diseases of Infants and Children.

Fifth Edition. Post 8vo, 8s. 6d.

A Practical Manual of the Diseases of Children.

With a Formulary. By EDWARD ELLIS, M.D., Fifth Edition. Crown 8vo, 10s.

A Manual for Hospital Nurses

and others engaged in Attending on the Sick, and a Glossary. By EDWARD J. DOMVILLE, Surgeon to the Exeter Lying-in Charity. Sixth Edition. Cr. 8vo, 2s. 6d.

A Manual of Nursing, Medical and Surgical.

By CHARLES J. CULLINGWORTH, M.D., Obstetric Physician to St. Thomas's Hospital. Second Edition. Fcap. 8vo, with Engravings, 3s. 6d.

By the same Author.

A Short Manual for Monthly Nurses.

Second Edition. Fcap. 8vo, 1s. 6d.

Hospital Sisters and their Duties.

By EVA C. E. LÜCKES, Matron to the London Hospital. Second Edition. Crown 8vo, 2s. 6d.

Diseases and their Commencement.
Lectures to Trained Nurses. By DONALD W. C. HOOD, M.D., M.R.C.P., Physician to the West London Hospital. Crown 8vo, 2s. 6d.

Outlines of Infectious Diseases:
For the use of Clinical Students. By J. W. ALLAN, M.B., Physician Superintendent Glasgow Fever Hospital. Fcap. 8vo., 3s.

Infant Feeding and its Influence on Life;
By C. H. F. ROUTH, M.D., Physician to the Samaritan Hospital. Fourth Edition. Fcap. 8vo. [*Preparing.*

Manual of Botany:
Including the Structure, Classification, Properties, Uses, and Functions of Plants. By ROBERT BENTLEY, Professor of Botany in King's College and to the Pharmaceutical Society. Fifth Edition. Crown 8vo, with 1,178 Engravings, 15s.

By the same Author.

The Student's Guide to Structural, Morphological, and Physiological Botany.
With 660 Engravings. Fcap. 8vo, 7s. 6d.

Also.

The Student's Guide to Systematic Botany,
including the Classification of Plants and Descriptive Botany. Fcap. 8vo, with 350 Engravings, 3s. 6d.

Medicinal Plants:
Being descriptions, with original figures, of the Principal Plants employed in Medicine, and an account of their Properties and Uses. By Prof. BENTLEY and Dr. H. TRIMEN, F.R.S. In 4 vols., large 8vo, with 306 Coloured Plates, bound in Half Morocco, Gilt Edges, £11 11s.

Materia Medica.
A Manual for the use of Students. By ISAMBARD OWEN, M.D., F.R.C.P., Lecturer on Materia Medica, &c., to St. George's Hospital. Second Edition. Crown 8vo, 6s. 6d.

Royle's Manual of Materia Medica and Therapeutics.
Sixth Edition, including additions and alterations in the B.P. 1885. By JOHN HARLEY, M.D., Physician to St. Thomas's Hospital. Crown 8vo, with 139 Engravings, 15s.

Materia Medica and Therapeutics:
Vegetable Kingdom — Organic Compounds — Animal Kingdom. By CHARLES D. F. PHILLIPS, M.D., F.R.S. Edin., late Lecturer on Materia Medica and Therapeutics at the Westminster Hospital Medical School. 8vo, 25s.

The Student's Guide to Materia Medica and Therapeutics.
By JOHN C. THOROWGOOD, M.D., F.R.C.P. Second Edition. Fcap. 8vo, 7s.

A Companion to the British Pharmacopœia.
By PETER SQUIRE, Revised by his Sons, P. W. and A. H. SQUIRE. 14th Edition. 8vo, 10s. 6d.

By the same Authors.

The Pharmacopœias of the London Hospitals,
arranged in Groups for Easy Reference and Comparison. Fifth Edition. 18mo, 6s.

The Prescriber's Pharmacopœia:
The Medicines arranged in Classes according to their Action, with their Composition and Doses. By NESTOR J. C. TIRARD, M.D., F.R.C.P., Professor of Materia Medica and Therapeutics in King's College, London. Sixth Edition. 32mo, bound in leather, 3s.

A Treatise on the Principles and Practice of Medicine.
Sixth Edition. By AUSTIN FLINT, M.D., W.H. WELCH, M.D., and AUSTIN FLINT, jun., M.D. 8vo, with Engravings, 26s.

Climate and Fevers of India,
with a series of Cases (Croonian Lectures, 1882). By Sir JOSEPH FAYRER, K.C.S.I., M.D. 8vo, with 17 Temperature Charts, 12s.

By the same Author.

The Natural History and Epidemiology of Cholera:
Being the Annual Oration of the Medical Society of London, 1888. 8vo, 3s. 6d.

Family Medicine for India.
A Manual. By WILLIAM J. MOORE, M.D., C.I.E., Honorary Surgeon to the Viceroy of India. Published under the Authority of the Government of India. Fifth Edition. Post 8vo, with Engravings. [*In the Press.*

By the same Author.

A Manual of the Diseases of India:
With a Compendium of Diseases generally. Second Edition. Post 8vo, 10s.

The Prevention of Disease in Tropical and Sub-Tropical Campaigns.
(Parkes Memorial Prize for 1886.) By ANDREW DUNCAN, M.D., B.S. Lond., F.R.C.S., Surgeon, Bengal Army. 8vo, 12s. 6d.

Practical Therapeutics:
A Manual. By EDWARD J. WARING, C.I.E., M.D., F.R.C.P., and DUDLEY W. BUXTON, M.D., B.S. Lond. Fourth Edition. Crown 8vo, 14s.

By the same Author.

Bazaar Medicines of India,
And Common Medical Plants: With Full Index of Diseases, indicating their Treatment by these and other Agents procurable throughout India, &c. Fourth Edition. Fcap. 8vo, 5s.

A Commentary on the Diseases of India. By NORMAN CHEVERS, C.I.E., M.D., F.R.C.S., Deputy Surgeon-General H.M. Indian Army. 8vo, 24s.

The Principles and Practice of Medicine. By C. HILTON FAGGE, M.D. Second Edition. Edited by P. H. PYE-SMITH, M.D., F.R.S., F.R.C.P., Physician to, and Lecturer on Medicine in, Guy's Hospital. 2 vols. 8vo. Cloth, 38s.; Half Leather, 44s.

The Student's Guide to the Practice of Medicine. By M. CHARTERIS, M.D., Professor of Therapeutics and Materia Medica in the University of Glasgow. Fifth Edition. Fcap. 8vo, with Engravings on Copper and Wood, 9s.

Hooper's Physicians' Vade-Mecum. A Manual of the Principles and Practice of Physic. Tenth Edition. By W. A. GUY, F.R.C.P., F.R.S., and J. HARLEY, M.D., F.R.C.P. With 118 Engravings. Fcap. 8vo, 12s. 6d.

Preventive Medicine. Collected Essays. By WILLIAM SQUIRE, M.D., F.R.C.P., Physician to St. George, Hanover-square, Dispensary. 8vo, 6s. 6d.

The Student's Guide to Clinical Medicine and Case-Taking. By FRANCIS WARNER, M.D., F.R.C.P., Physician to the London Hospital. Second Edition. Fcap. 8vo, 5s.

An Atlas of the Pathological Anatomy of the Lungs. By the late WILSON FOX, F.R.C.P., Physician to H.M. the Queen. With 45 Plates (mostly Coloured) and Engravings. 4to, half-bound in Calf, 70s.

The Student's Guide to Diseases of the Chest. By VINCENT D. HARRIS, M.D. Lond., F.R.C.P., Physician to the City of London Hospital for Diseases of the Chest, Victoria Park. Fcap. 8vo, with 55 Illustrations (some Coloured), 7s. 6d.

How to Examine the Chest: A Practical Guide for the use of Students. By SAMUEL WEST, M.D., F.R.C.P., Physician to the City of London Hospital for Diseases of the Chest; Assistant Physician to St. Bartholomew's Hospital. With 42 Engravings. Fcap. 8vo, 5s.

Contributions to Clinical and Practical Medicine. By A. T. HOUGHTON WATERS, M.D., Physician to the Liverpool Royal Infirmary. 8vo, with Engravings, 7s.

Fever: A Clinical Study. By T. J. MACLAGAN, M.D. 8vo, 7s. 6d.

The Student's Guide to Medical Diagnosis. By SAMUEL FENWICK, M.D., F.R.C.P., Physician to the London Hospital, and BEDFORD FENWICK, M.D., M.R.C.P. Sixth Edition. 8vo, with 114 Engravings, 7s.

By the same Author.

The Student's Outlines of Medical Treatment. Second Edition. Fcap. 8vo, 7s.

Also.

On Chronic Atrophy of the Stomach, and on the Nervous Affections of the Digestive Organs. 8vo, 8s.

Also.

The Saliva as a Test for Functional Diseases of the Liver. Crown 8vo, 2s.

The Microscope in Medicine. By LIONEL S. BEALE, M.B., F.R.S., Physician to King's College Hospital. Fourth Edition. 8vo, with 86 Plates, 21s.

Also.

On Slight Ailments: Their Nature and Treatment. Second Edition. 8vo, 5s.

Medical Lectures and Essays. By G. JOHNSON, M.D., F.R.C.P., F.R.S., Consulting Physician to King's College Hospital. 8vo, with 46 Engravings, 25s.

Notes on Asthma: Its Forms and Treatment. By JOHN C. THOROWGOOD, M.D., Physician to the Hospital for Diseases of the Chest. Third Edition. Crown 8vo, 4s. 6d.

Winter Cough (Catarrh, Bronchitis, Emphysema, Asthma). By HORACE DOBELL, M.D., Consulting Physician to the Royal Hospital for Diseases of the Chest. Third Edition. 8vo, with Coloured Plates, 10s. 6d.

By the same Author.

Loss of Weight, Blood-Spitting, and Lung Disease. Second Edition. 8vo, with Chromo-lithograph, 10s. 6d.

Also.

The Mont Dore Cure, and the Proper Way to Use it. 8vo, 7s. 6d.

Vaccinia and Variola: A Study of their Life History. By JOHN B. BUIST, M.D., F.R.S.E., Teacher of Vaccination for the Local Government Board. Crown 8vo, with 24 Coloured Plates, 7s. 6d.

Treatment of Some of the Forms of Valvular Disease of the Heart. By A. E. SANSOM, M.D., F.R.C.P., Physician to the London Hospital. Second Edition. Fcap. 8vo, with 26 Engravings, 4s. 6d.

Diseases of the Heart and Aorta:
Clinical Lectures. By G. W. BALFOUR, M.D., F.R.C.P., F.R.S. Edin., late Senior Physician and Lecturer on Clinical Medicine, Royal Infirmary, Edinburgh. Second Edition. 8vo, with Chromo-lithograph and Wood Engravings, 12s. 6d.

Medical Ophthalmoscopy:
A Manual and Atlas. By W. R. GOWERS, M.D., F.R.C.P., F.R.S., Professor of Clinical Medicine in University College, Physician to University College Hospital and to the National Hospital for the Paralyzed and Epileptic. Second Edition, with Coloured Plates and Woodcuts. 8vo, 18s.

By the same Author.

Diagnosis of Diseases of the Brain. Second Edition. 8vo, with Engravings, 7s. 6d.

Also.

Diagnosis of Diseases of the Spinal Cord. Third Edition. 8vo, with Engravings, 4s. 6d.

Also,

A Manual of Diseases of the Nervous System.
Vol. I. Diseases of the Spinal Cord and Nerves. Roy. 8vo, with 171 Engravings (many figures), 12s. 6d.
Vol. II. Diseases of the Brain and Cranial Nerves: General and Functional Diseases of the Nervous System. 8vo, with 170 Engravings, 17s. 6d.

Diseases of the Nervous System.
Lectures delivered at Guy's Hospital. By SAMUEL WILKS, M.D., F.R.S. Second Edition. 8vo, 18s.

Nerve Vibration and Excitation, as Agents in the Treatment of Functional Disorder and Organic Disease. By J. MORTIMER GRANVILLE, M.D. 8vo, 5s.

By the same Author.

Gout in its Clinical Aspects.
Crown 8vo, 6s.

Regimen to be adopted in Cases of Gout. By WILHELM EBSTEIN, M.D., Professor of Clinical Medicine in Göttingen. Translated by JOHN SCOTT, M.A., M.B. 8vo, 2s. 6d.

Diseases of the Nervous System.
Clinical Lectures. By THOMAS BUZZARD, M.D., F.R.C.P., Physician to the National Hospital for the Paralysed and Epileptic. With Engravings, 8vo. 15s.

By the same Author.

Some Forms of Paralysis from Peripheral Neuritis: of Gouty, Alcoholic, Diphtheritic, and other origin. Crown 8vo, 5s.

Diseases of the Liver:
With and without Jaundice. By GEORGE HARLEY, M.D., F.R.C.P., F.R.S. 8vo, with 2 Plates and 36 Engravings, 21s.

By the same Author.

Inflammations of the Liver, and their Sequelæ. Crown 8vo, with Engravings, 5s.

Gout, Rheumatism,
And the Allied Affections; with Chapters on Longevity and Sleep. By PETER HOOD, M.D. Third Edition. Crown 8vo, 7s. 6d.

Diseases of the Stomach:
The Varieties of Dyspepsia, their Diagnosis and Treatment. By S. O. HABERSHON, M.D., F.R.C.P. Third Edition. Crown 8vo, 5s.

By the same Author.

Pathology of the Pneumo-
gastric Nerve: Lumleian Lectures for 1876. Second Edition. Post 8vo, 4s.

Also.

Diseases of the Abdomen,
Comprising those of the Stomach and other parts of the Alimentary Canal, Œsophagus, Cæcum, Intestines, and Peritoneum. Fourth Edition. 8vo, with 5 Plates, 21s.

Also.

Diseases of the Liver,
Their Pathology and Treatment. Lettsomian Lectures. Second Edition. Post 8vo, 4s.

On the Relief of Excessive and Dangerous Tympanites by Puncture of the Abdomen. By JOHN W. OGLE, M.A., M.D., F.R.C.P., Consulting Physician to St. George's Hospital. 8vo, 5s. 6d.

Acute Intestinal Strangulation,
And Chronic Intestinal Obstruction (Mode of Death from). By THOMAS BRYANT, F.R.C.S., Senior Surgeon to Guy's Hospital. 8vo, 3s.

A Treatise on the Diseases of the Nervous System. By JAMES ROSS, M.D., F.R.C.P., Assistant Physician to the Manchester Royal Infirmary. Second Edition. 2 vols. 8vo, with Lithographs, Photographs, and 332 Woodcuts, 52s. 6d.

By the same Author.

Handbook of the Diseases of the Nervous System. Roy. 8vo, with 184 Engravings, 18s.

Also.

Aphasia:
Being a Contribution to the Subject of the Dissolution of Speech from Cerebral Disease. 8vo, with Engravings, 4s. 6d.

Spasm in Chronic Nerve Disease.

(Gulstonian Lectures.) By SEYMOUR J. SHARKEY, M.A., M.B., F.R.C.P., Assistant Physician to, and Joint Lecturer on Pathology at, St. Thomas's Hospital. 8vo, with Engravings, 5s.

Food and Dietetics,

Physiologically and Therapeutically Considered. By F. W. PAVY, M.D., F.R.S., Physician to Guy's Hospital. · Second Edition. 8vo, 15s.

By the same Author.

Croonian Lectures on Certain

Points connected with Diabetes. 8vo, 4s. 6d.

Headaches :

Their Nature, Causes, and Treatment. By W. H. DAY, M.D., Physician to the Samaritan Hospital. Fourth Edition. Crown 8vo, with Engravings, 7s. 6d.

Health Resorts at Home and

Abroad. By M. CHARTERIS, M.D., Professor of Therapeutics and Materia Medica in the University of Glasgow. Second Edition. Crown 8vo, with Map, 5s. 6d.

Winter and Spring

On the Shores of the Mediterranean. By HENRY BENNET, M.D. Fifth Edition. Post 8vo, with numerous Plates, Maps, and Engravings, 12s. 6d.

Medical Guide to the Mineral

Waters of France and its Wintering Stations. With a Special Map. By A. VINTRAS, M.D., Physician to the French Embassy, and to the French Hospital, London. Crown 8vo, 8s.

The Ocean as a Health-Resort :

A Practical Handbook of the Sea, for the use of Tourists and Health-Seekers. By WILLIAM S. WILSON, L.R.C.P. Second Edition, with Chart of Ocean Routes, &c. Crown 8vo, 7s. 6d.

Ambulance Handbook for Volunteers and Others.

By J. ARDAVON RAYE, L.K. & Q.C.P.I., L.R.C.S.I., late Surgeon to H.B.M. Transport No. 14, Zulu Campaign, and Surgeon E.I.R. Rifles. 8vo, with 16 Plates (50 figures), 3s. 6d.

Ambulance Lectures :

To which is added a NURSING LECTURE. By JOHN M. H. MARTIN, Honorary Surgeon to the Blackburn Infirmary. Second Edition. Crown 8vo, with 59 Engravings, 2s.

Commoner Diseases and Accidents to Life and Limb:

their Prevention and Immediate Treatment. By M. M. BASIL, M.A., M.B., C.M. Crown 8vo, 2s. 6d.

How to Use a Galvanic Battery

in Medicine and Surgery. By HERBERT TIBBITS, M.D., F.R.C.P.E., Senior Physician to the West London Hospital for Paralysis and Epilepsy. Third Edition. 8vo, with Engravings, 4s.

By the same Author.

A Map of Ziemssen's Motor

Points of the Human Body : A Guide to Localised Electrisation. Mounted on Rollers, 35 × 21. With 20 Illustrations, 5s.   *Also.*

Electrical and Anatomical Demonstrations.

A Handbook for Trained Nurses and Masseuses. Crown 8vo, with 44 Illustrations, 5s.

Also

Massage and Allied Modes of

Treatment. With 46 Engravings. 8vo, 4s. 6d.

Surgical Emergencies :

Together with the Emergencies attendant on Parturition and the Treatment of Poisoning. By W. PAUL SWAIN, F.R.C.S., Surgeon to the South Devon and East Cornwall Hospital. Fourth Edition. Crown 8vo, with 120 Engravings, 5s.

Operative Surgery in the Calcutta Medical College Hospital.

Statistics, Cases, and Comments. By KENNETH MCLEOD, A.M., M.D., F.R.C.S.E., Surgeon-Major, Indian Medical Service, Professor of Surgery in Calcutta Medical College. 8vo, with Illustrations, 12s. 6d.

A Course of Operative Surgery.

By CHRISTOPHER HEATH, Surgeon to University College Hospital. Second Edition. With 20 coloured Plates (180 figures) from Nature, by M. LÉVEILLÉ, and several Woodcuts. Large 8vo, 30s.

By the same Author.

The Student's Guide to Surgical

Diagnosis. Second Edition. Fcap. 8vo, 6s. 6d.   *Also.*

Manual of Minor Surgery and

Bandaging. For the use of House-Surgeons, Dressers, and Junior Practitioners. Eighth Edition. Fcap. 8vo, with 142 Engravings, 6s.

Also.

Injuries and Diseases of the

Jaws. Third Edition. 8vo, with Plate and 206 Wood Engravings, 14s.

Also,

Lectures on Certain Diseases

of the Jaws. Delivered at the R.C.S., Eng., 1887. 8vo, with 64 Engravings, 2s. 6d.

The Practice of Surgery:

A Manual. By THOMAS BRYANT, Consulting Surgeon to Guy's Hospital. Fourth Edition. 2 vols. crown 8vo, with 750 Engravings (many being coloured), and including 6 chromo plates, 32s.

By the same Author.

On Tension : Inflammation of Bone, and Head Injuries. Hunterian Lectures, 1888. 8vo, 6s.

Surgery: its Theory and Practice (Student's Guide). By WILLIAM J. WALSHAM, F.R.C.S., Assistant Surgeon to St. Bartholomew's Hospital. Fcap. 8vo, with 236 Engravings, 10s. 6d.

The Surgeon's Vade-Mecum :

A Manual of Modern Surgery. By R. DRUITT, F.R.C.S. Twelfth Edition. By STANLEY BOYD, M.B., F.R.C.S. Assistant Surgeon and Pathologist to Charing Cross Hospital. Crown 8vo, with 373 Engravings 16s.

Surgical Pathology and Morbid Anatomy (Student's Guide). By ANTHONY A. BOWLBY, F.R.C.S., Surgical Registrar and Demonstrator of Surgical Pathology to St. Bartholomew's Hospital. Fcap. 8vo, with 135 Engravings, 9s.

Regional Surgery :

Including Surgical Diagnosis. A Manual for the use of Students. By F. A. SOUTHAM, M.A., M.B., F.R.C.S., Assistant Surgeon to the Manchester Royal Infirmary. Part I. The Head and Neck. Crown 8vo, 6s. 6d. — Part II. The Upper Extremity and Thorax. Crown 8vo, 7s. 6d. Part III. The Abdomen and Lower Extremity. Crown 8vo, 7s.

A Treatise on Dislocations.

By LEWIS A. STIMSON, M.D., Professor of Clinical Surgery in the University of the City of New York. Roy. 8vo, with 163 Engravings, 15s.

By the same Author.

A Treatise on Fractures.

Roy. 8vo, with 360 Engravings, 21s.

Lectures on Orthopædic Surgery. By BERNARD E. BRODHURST, F.R.C.S., Surgeon to the Royal Orthopædic Hospital. Second Edition. 8vo, with Engravings, 12s. 6d.

By the same Author.

On Anchylosis, and the Treatment for the Removal of Deformity and the Restoration of Mobility in Various Joints. Fourth Edition. 8vo, with Engravings, 5s.

Also.

Curvatures and Disease of the Spine. Fourth Edition. 8vo, with Engravings, 7s. 6d.

Illustrations of Clinical Surgery.

By JONATHAN HUTCHINSON, F.R.S., Senior Surgeon to the London Hospital. In fasciculi. 6s. 6d each. Fasc. I. to X. bound, with Appendix and Index, £3 10s. Fasc. XI. to XXIII. bound, with Index, £4 10s.

Diseases of Bones and Joints.

By CHARLES MACNAMARA, F.R.C.S., Surgeon to, and Lecturer on Surgery at, the Westminster Hospital. 8vo, with Plates and Engravings, 12s.

Injuries of the Spine and Spinal Cord, and NERVOUS SHOCK, in their Surgical and Medico-Legal Aspects. By HERBERT W. PAGE, M.C. Cantab., F.R.C.S., Surgeon to St. Mary's Hospital. Second Edition, post 8vo, 10s.

Spina Bifida :

Its Treatment by a New Method. By JAS. MORTON, M.D., L.R.C.S.E., Professor of Materia Medica in Anderson's College, Glasgow. 8vo, with Plates, 7s. 6d.

Face and Foot Deformities.

By FREDERICK CHURCHILL, C.M., Surgeon to the Victoria Hospital for Children. 8vo, with Plates and Illustrations, 10s. 6d.

Clubfoot :

Its Causes, Pathology, and Treatment. By WM. ADAMS, F.R.C.S., Surgeon to the Great Northern Hospital. Second Edition. 8vo, with 106 Engravings and 6 Lithographic Plates, 15s.

By the same Author.

On Contraction of the Fingers, and its Treatment by Subcutaneous Operation ; and on Obliteration of Depressed Cicatrices, by the same Method. 8vo, with 30 Engravings, 4s. 6d.

Also.

Lateral and other Forms of Curvature of the Spine : Their Pathology and Treatment. Second Edition. 8vo, with 5 Lithographic Plates and 72 Wood Engravings, 10s. 6d.

Electricity and its Manner of Working in the Treatment of Disease. By WM. E. STEAVENSON, M.D., Physician and Electrician to St. Bartholomew's Hospital. 8vo, 4s. 6d.

On Diseases and Injuries of the Eye : A Course of Systematic and Clinical Lectures to Students and Medical Practitioners. By J. R. WOLFE, M.D., F.R.C.S.E., Lecturer on Ophthalmic Medicine and Surgery in Anderson's College, Glasgow. With 10 Coloured Plates and 157 Wood Engravings. 8vo, £1 1s.

Hints on Ophthalmic Out-Patient Practice. By CHARLES HIGGENS, Ophthalmic Surgeon to Guy's Hospital. Third Edition. Fcap. 8vo, 3s.

The Student's Guide to Diseases

of the Eye. By EDWARD NETTLESHIP, F.R.C.S., Ophthalmic Surgeon to St. Thomas's Hospital. Fourth Edition. Fcap. 8vo, with 164 Engravings and a Set of Coloured Papers illustrating Colour-Blindness, 7s. 6d.

Manual of the Diseases of the

Eye. By CHARLES MACNAMARA, F.R.C.S., Surgeon to Westminster Hospital. Fourth Edition. Crown 8vo, with 4 Coloured Plates and 66 Engravings, 10s. 6d.

Normal and Pathological His-

tology of the Human Eye and Eyelids. By C. FRED. POLLOCK, M.D., F.R.C.S. and F.R.S.E., Surgeon for Diseases of the Eye to Anderson's College Dispensary, Glasgow. Crown 8vo, with 100 Plates (230 drawings), 15s.

Atlas of Ophthalmoscopy.

Composed of 12 Chromo-lithographic Plates (59 Figures drawn from nature) and Explanatory Text. By RICHARD LIEBREICH, M.R.C.S. Translated by H. ROSBOROUGH SWANZY, M.B. Third edition, 4to, 40s.

Refraction of the Eye:

A Manual for Students. By GUSTAVUS HARTRIDGE, F.R.C.S., Assistant Surgeon to the Royal Westminster Ophthalmic Hospital. Third Edition. Crown 8vo, with 96 Illustrations, Test-types, &c., 5s. 6d.

Squint:

(Clinical Investigations on). By C. SCHWEIGGER, M.D., Professor of Ophthalmology in the University of Berlin. Edited by GUSTAVUS HARTRIDGE, F.R.C.S. 8vo, 5s.

Practitioner's Handbook of

Diseases of the Ear and Naso-Pharynx. By H. MACNAUGHTON JONES, M.D., late Professor of the Queen's University in Ireland, Surgeon to the Cork Ophthalmic and Aural Hospital. Third Edition of "Aural Surgery." Roy. 8vo, with 128 Engravings, 6s.

By the same Author.

Atlas of Diseases of the Mem-

brana Tympani. In Coloured Plates, containing 62 Figures, with Text. Crown 4to, 21s.

Endemic Goitre or Thyreocele:

Its Etiology, Clinical Characters, Pathology, Distribution, Relations to Cretinism, Myxœdema, &c., and Treatment. By WILLIAM ROBINSON, M.D. 8vo, 5s.

Diseases and Injuries of the

Ear. By Sir WILLIAM B. DALBY, Aural Surgeon to St. George's Hospital. Third Edition. Crown 8vo, with Engravings, 7s. 6d.

By the Same Author.

Short Contributions to Aural

Surgery, between 1875 and 1886. 8vo, with Engravings, 3s. 6d.

Diseases of the Throat and

Nose: A Manual. By Sir MORELL MACKENZIE, M.D., Senior Physician to the Hospital for Diseases of the Throat. Vol. II. Diseases of the Nose and Naso-Pharynx ; with a Section on Diseases of the Œsophagus. Post 8vo, with 93 Engravings, 12s. 6d.

By the same Author.

Diphtheria:

Its Nature and Treatment, Varieties, and Local Expressions. 8vo, 5s.

Sore Throat:

Its Nature, Varieties, and Treatment. By PROSSER JAMES, M.D., Physician to the Hospital for Diseases of the Throat. Fifth Edition. Post 8vo, with Coloured Plates and Engravings, 6s. 6d.

Studies in Pathological Anatomy,

Especially in Relation to Laryngeal Neoplasms. By R. NORRIS WOLFENDEN, M.D., Senior Physician to the Throat Hospital, and SIDNEY MARTIN, M.D., Pathologist to the City of London Hospital, Victoria Park. I. Papilloma. Roy. 8vo, with Coloured Plates, 2s. 6d.

A System of Dental Surgery.

By Sir JOHN TOMES, F.R.S., and C. S. TOMES, M.A., F.R.S. Third Edition. Crown 8vo, with 292 Engravings, 15s.

Dental Anatomy, Human and

Comparative: A Manual. By CHARLES S. TOMES, M.A., F.R.S. Second Edition. Crown 8vo, with 191 Engravings, 12s. 6d.

The Student's Guide to Dental

Anatomy and Surgery. By HENRY SEWILL, M.R.C.S., L.D.S. Second Edition. Fcap. 8vo, with 78 Engravings, 5s. 6d.

A Manual of Nitrous Oxide

Anæsthesia, for the use of Students and General Practitioners. By J. FREDERICK W. SILK, M.D. Lond., M.R.C.S., Anæsthetist to the Great Northern Central Hospital, and to the National Dental Hospital. 8vo, with 26 Engravings, 5s.

Mechanical Dentistry in Gold

and Vulcanite. By F. H. BALKWILL, L.D.S.R.C.S. 8vo, with 2 Lithographic Plates and 57 Engravings, 10s.

Principles and Practice of Dentistry :

including Anatomy, Physiology, Pathology, Therapeutics, Dental Surgery, and Mechanism. By C. A. HARRIS, M.D., D.D.S. Edited by F. J. S. GORGAS, A.M., M.D., D.D.S., Professor in the Dental Department of Maryland University. Eleventh Edition. 8vo, with 750 Illustrations, 31s. 6d.

A Practical Treatise on Mechanical Dentistry.

By JOSEPH RICHARDSON, M.D., D.D.S., late Emeritus Professor of Prosthetic Dentistry in the Indiana Medical College. Fourth Edition. Roy. 8vo, with 458 Engravings, 21s.

Elements of Dental Materia Medica and Therapeutics, with Pharmacopœia.

By JAMES STOCKEN, L.D.S.R.C.S., Pereira Prizeman for Materia Medica, and THOMAS GADDES, L.D.S. Eng. and Edin. Third Edition. Fcap. 8vo, 7s. 6d.

Atlas of Skin Diseases.

By TILBURY FOX, M.D., F.R.C.P. With 72 Coloured Plates. Royal 4to, half morocco, £6 6s.

Diseases of the Skin :

With an Analysis of 8,000 Consecutive Cases and a Formulary. By L. D. BULKLEY, M.D., Physician for Skin Diseases at the New York Hospital. Crown 8vo, 6s. 6d.

By the same Author.

Acne : its Etiology, Pathology, and Treatment :

Based upon a Study of 1,500 Cases. 8vo, with Engravings, 10s.

On Certain Rare Diseases of the Skin.

By JONATHAN HUTCHINSON, F.R.S., Senior Surgeon to the London Hospital, and to the Hospital for Diseases of the Skin. 8vo, 10s. 6d.

Diseases of the Skin :

A Practical Treatise for the Use of Students and Practitioners. By J. N. HYDE, A.M., M.D., Professor of Skin and Venereal Diseases, Rush Medical College, Chicago. Second Edition. 8vo, with 2 Coloured Plates and 96 Engravings, 20s.

Parasites :

A Treatise on the Entozoa of Man and Animals, including some Account of the Ectozoa. By T. SPENCER COBBOLD, M.D., F.R.S. 8vo, with 85 Engravings, 15s.

Manual of Animal Vaccination,

preceded by Considerations on Vaccination in general. By E. WARLOMONT, M.D., Founder of the State Vaccine Institute of Belgium. Translated and edited by ARTHUR J. HARRIES, M.D. Crown 8vo, 4s. 6d.

Leprosy in British Guiana.

By JOHN D. HILLIS, F.R.C.S., M.R.I.A., Medical Superintendent of the Leper Asylum, British Guiana. Imp. 8vo, with 22 Lithographic Coloured Plates and Wood Engravings, £1 11s. 6d.

Cancer of the Breast.

By THOMAS W. NUNN, F.R.C.S., Consulting Surgeon to the Middlesex Hospital. 4to, with 21 Coloured Plates, £2 2s.

On Cancer :

Its Allies, and other Tumours; their Medical and Surgical Treatment. By F. A. PURCELL, M.D., M.C., Surgeon to the Cancer Hospital, Brompton. 8vo, with 21 Engravings, 10s. 6d.

Sarcoma and Carcinoma :

Their Pathology, Diagnosis, and Treatment. By HENRY T. BUTLIN, F.R.C.S., Assistant Surgeon to St. Bartholomew's Hospital. 8vo, with 4 Plates, 8s.

By the same Author.

Malignant Disease of the Larynx (Sarcoma and Carcinoma).

8vo, with 5 Engravings, 5s.

Also.

Operative Surgery of Malignant Disease.

8vo, 14s.

Cancerous Affections of the Skin.

(Epithelioma and Rodent Ulcer.) By GEORGE THIN, M.D. Post 8vo, with 8 Engravings, 5s.

By the same Author.

Pathology and Treatment of Ringworm.

8vo, with 21 Engravings, 5s.

Cancer of the Mouth, Tongue, and Alimentary Tract :

their Pathology, Symptoms, Diagnosis, and Treatment. By FREDERIC B. JESSETT, F.R.C.S., Surgeon to the Cancer Hospital, Brompton. 8vo, 10s.

Lectures on the Surgical Disorders of the Urinary Organs.

By REGINALD HARRISON, F.R.C.S., Surgeon to the Liverpool Royal Infirmary. Third Edition, with 117 Engravings. 8vo, 12s. 6d.

Hydrocele :

Its several Varieties and their Treatment. By SAMUEL OSBORN, late Surgical Registrar to St. Thomas's Hospital. Fcap. 8vo, with Engravings, 3s.

By the same Author.

Diseases of the Testis.

Fcap. 8vo, with Engravings, 3s. 6d.

Diseases of the Urinary Organs.
Clinical Lectures. By Sir HENRY THOMPSON, F.R.C.S., Emeritus Professor of Clinical Surgery and Consulting Surgeon to University College Hospital. Eighth Edition. 8vo, with 121 Engravings, 10s. 6d.

By the same Author.

Diseases of the Prostate :
Their Pathology and Treatment. Sixth Edition. 8vo, with 39 Engravings, 6s.

Also.

Surgery of the Urinary Organs.
Some Important Points connected therewith. Lectures delivered in the R.C.S. 8vo, with 44 Engravings. Students' Edition, 2s. 6d.

Also.

Practical Lithotomy and Lithotrity; or, An Inquiry into the Best Modes of Removing Stone from the Bladder. Third Edition. 8vo, with 87 Engravings, 10s. *Also.*

The Preventive Treatment of Calculous Disease, and the Use of Solvent Remedies. Third Edition. Crown 8vo, 2s. 6d.

Also.

Tumours of the Bladder:
Their Nature, Symptoms, and Surgical Treatment. 8vo, with numerous Illustrations, 5s.

Also.

Stricture of the Urethra, and Urinary Fistulæ: their Pathology and Treatment. Fourth Edition. With 74 Engravings. 8vo, 6s.

Also.

The Suprapubic Operation of Opening the Bladder for the Stone and for Tumours. 8vo, with 14 Engravings, 3s. 6d.

Electric Illumination of the Male Bladder and Urethra, as a Means of Diagnosis of Obscure Vesico-Urethral Diseases. By E. HURRY FENWICK, F.R.C.S., Assistant Surgeon to the London Hospital and Surgeon to St. Peter's Hospital for Stone. 8vo, with 30 Engravings, 4s. 6d.

Modern Treatment of Stone in the Bladder by Litholopaxy. By P. J. FREYER, M.A., M.D., M.Ch., Bengal Medical Service. 8vo, with Engravings, 5s.

The Surgical Diseases of the Genito - Urinary Organs, including Syphilis. By E. L. KEYES, M.D., Professor of Genito-Urinary Surgery, Syphiology, and Dermatology in Bellevue Hospital Medical College, New York (a revision of VAN BUREN and KEYES' Text-book). Roy. 8vo, with 114 Engravings, 21s.

The Surgery of the Rectum.
By HENRY SMITH, Emeritus Professor of Surgery in King's College, Consulting Surgeon to the Hospital. Fifth Edition. 8vo, 6s.

Diseases of the Rectum and Anus. By W. HARRISON CRIPPS, F.R.C.S., Assistant Surgeon to St. Bartholomew's Hospital, &c. 8vo, with 13 Lithographic Plates and numerous Wood Engravings, 12s. 6d.

Urinary and Renal Derangements and Calculous Disorders.
By LIONEL S. BEALE, F.R.C.P., F.R.S., Physician to King's College Hospital. 8vo, 5s.

The Diagnosis and Treatment of Diseases of the Rectum. By WILLIAM ALLINGHAM, F.R.C.S., Surgeon to St. Mark's Hospital for Fistula. Fifth Edition. By HERBERT WM. ALLINGHAM, F.R.C.S., Surgeon to the Great Northern Central Hospital, Demonstrator of Anatomy at St. George's Hospital. 8vo, with 53 Engravings. 10s. 6d.

Syphilis and Pseudo-Syphilis.
By ALFRED COOPER, F.R.C.S., Surgeon to the Lock Hospital, to St. Mark's and the West London Hospitals. 8vo, 10s. 6d.

Diagnosis and Treatment of Syphilis. By TOM ROBINSON, M.D., Physician to St. John's Hospital for Diseases of the Skin. Crown 8vo, 3s. 6d.

By the same Author.

Eczema : its Etiology, Pathology, and Treatment. Crown 8vo, 3s. 6d.

Coulson on Diseases of the Bladder and Prostate Gland. Sixth Edition. By WALTER J. COULSON, Surgeon to the Lock Hospital and to St. Peter's Hospital for Stone. 8vo, 16s.

The Medical Adviser in Life Assurance. By Sir E. H. SIEVEKING, M.D., F.R.C.P. Second Edition. Crown 8vo, 6s.

A Medical Vocabulary :
An Explanation of all Terms and Phrases used in the various Departments of Medical Science and Practice, their Derivation, Meaning, Application, and Pronunciation. By R. G. MAYNE, M.D., LL.D. Sixth Edition. [*In the Press.*

A Dictionary of Medical Science:
Containing a concise Explanation of the various Subjects and Terms of Medicine, &c. By ROBLEY DUNGLISON, M.D. LL.D. Royal 8vo, 28s.

INDEX.

[Continued on the next page.

The following CATALOGUES issued by J. & A. CHURCHILL will be forwarded post free on application :—

A. *J. & A. Churchill's General List of about* 650 *works on Anatomy, Physiology, Hygiene, Midwifery, Materia Medica, Medicine, Surgery, Chemistry, Botany, &c., &c., with a complete Index to their Subjects, for easy reference.* N.B.—*This List includes* B, C, & D.

B. *Selection from J. & A. Churchill's General List, comprising all recent Works published by them on the Art and Science of Medicine.*

C. *J. & A. Churchill' Catalogue of Text Books specially arranged for Students.*

D. *A selected and descriptive List of J. & A. Churchill's Works on Chemistry, Materia Medica, Pharmacy, Botany, Photography, Zoology, the Microscope, and other branches of Science.*

E. *The Medical Intelligencer, being a List of New Works and New Editions published by J. & A. Churchill.*

[Sent yearly to every Medical Practitioner in the United Kingdom whose name and address can be ascertained. A large number are also sent to the United States of America, Continental Europe, India, and the Colonies.]

AMERICA.—*J. & A. Churchill being in constant communication with various publishing houses in Boston, New York, and Philadelphia, are able, notwithstanding the absence of international copyright, to conduct negotiations favourable to English Authors.*

LONDON: 11, NEW BURLINGTON STREET.

Pardon & Sons, Printers,]   [*Wine Office Court, Fleet Street, E.C.*

www.ingramcontent.com/pod-product-compliance
Lightning Source LLC
Chambersburg PA
CBHW032355020726
47499CB00008B/2754